Singleish
By Elizabeth Butts
Distributed by Amazon.com and CreateSpace.com

This book is dedicated with so much love to my amazing husband, Mike; my wonderful parents and to a wonderful friend/author who gave me a much needed kick in the butt, A.E. Murphy.

Prologue

He slowly pulled at the strings on her chemise, lowering it off her shoulders, gently kissing her skin as it was exposed to him. A shudder ran through her, though whether from the cold or his attention, she would never know. He caressed her skin, his fingers soft as a breeze against her hardening nipple. She heard a moan and was embarrassed when she realized it came from her own throat. "Miranda," Ian purred, "you needn't be shy with me. I love you." "Oh, Ian, I can't believe that my boss expects me to work every Saturday without a promotion or raise in sight".

Wait... What? I blinked my eyes a few times. When did Miranda start speaking in my head in a male voice? A male voice that sounded suspiciously like...oh, shit. I looked up from my Kindle where Ian and Miranda were about to get all kilt freaky and into the eyes of my boyfriend of three years, Craig, who was looking at me expectantly. I wondered how long he'd been talking to me. I wondered if my subconscious had heard any of it. I closed my eyes a minute, mentally going over the last few minutes. Nope, nothing there. Just Scottish lairds and soft caresses. I wondered if he realized that I hadn't heard a word that he'd said. I risked a glance at him and saw a slightly reddening face and narrowed eyes. Um, yup. He knew. Crap.

I wished I could just go back to my Kindle, re-enter the world that demanded nothing of me. I mean, it was my day off...I should be able to sit on a couch and just lose myself in that world that existed within its electronic pages. However, reality called. I groaned inwardly, pushed the button to put my Kindle to sleep and turned and face the music.

"I'm sorry, honey, you know how I can get when I read. Could you repeat what you said?"

"Seriously? Again? I have been talking to you for the last ten minutes. You're trying to tell me that you haven't heard a damn word I've said for ten minutes?" Craig looked like he was about to spontaneously combust. Eek.

Inwardly I shuddered to think that I'd managed to zone out that completely, but didn't let him see.

"Hey, I've told you not to try to talk to me when I'm reading. You've been warned. If you see me on the couch with a Kindle, I'm really not there. It's just a shell, an illusion."

Uh-oh. I think that might have been the wrong thing to say. Was it possible that his hair was starting to singe? I squinted a little, yup… I'm pretty sure he was so mad that his hair was burning.

"Ash, that's it. I can't do this anymore. I can't compete with your warriors, squires, princes and lairds anymore. I don't wear a kilt. I don't have any 'shining armor'." I started to glaze over a bit when I pictured him in a kilt or in 'shining armor'. Wrong move. Focus!

"I am your real boyfriend, I'm here, but you can't be bothered with me because you'd rather be in a book. I need a break from this. I'm done"

I blinked my eyes a few times, my jaw on the ground as I watched him turn, stalk towards the door and slowly, quietly walk out the door and out of us. I glared at my Kindle, but I couldn't be too angry at it, because it was a really good story. But, what the hell did he mean by a 'break'? This was a little too Ross and Rachel from the 1990's.

I got up from the couch and ran out the door, stumbled down the steps and managed to make it to his car before he pulled out of the driveway. My chest was heaving from the exertion of running after him. I asked, "What…do you mean…that you're done? It…was just…a book."

He looked at me, his brown eyes soft and sad. "Ashley, this is the tip of the iceberg. I just feel like you don't have much more going on than going to work and vegging on the weekends. We don't do anything anymore. We don't go anywhere. Do you even want to be with me anymore? Do you even notice that I'm at your house almost every night? You just seem to want to work during the week and read on the weekend. I love you, I love you so damn much, but I don't know if it is enough for me to play second fiddle to electronics. I don't know if 'done' is the right thing to say, but I definitely need a breather."

With that lovely monologue, he put the car in reverse.

Chapter 1

So when you'd had so much of your life mapped out in your mind, and it just disappears in a moment, it was a little hard to readjust, you know? I mean, I guess I had just figured we were a forever sort of thing, so I was really surprised that he just walked away like that. Craig leaving, well, it hurt. I replayed the parting words over and over again, just trying to figure out what I missed, what went wrong.

Was I so horrible at reading body language that I didn't know he felt alone in our relationship? Had I really chosen my Kindle over him? If I couldn't figure out that my boyfriend is feeling neglected, I obviously have the social prowess of a slug. I probably shouldn't be allowed to interact with people at all.

It was kind of weird, I should be angry, throwing things. I just got sort of broken up with but not quite. I mean, did this mean that I've become so boring a person that I wasn't even exciting enough to fully break up with? I felt completely broken that he left, but I guess I was also feeling...I don't know...contemplative? Hmmmm, contemplative. I tried that word out in my mind. I then said it out loud. Yeah, that was about right. I was feeling contemplative.

I thought about calling my mom, to let her know we broke up, maybe cry on her shoulder or something. But knowing mom, she'd let me know that she was glad he was gone. She would tell me that she had never liked him anyway, he wasn't good enough for me yada, yada, yada. Even though she always asked if he could come to family gatherings before she even thought to ask me if I was interested. Seriously, there were times we'd be hanging out and he'd get a text from her asking him to come to a cook-out, and after he said he would, I'd get a text letting me know about the cook-out. Sheesh! He was a bit of a suck up – loved mom's cooking. Then again, I didn't know a soul in the world that didn't love my mom's cooking. It was redonkaballs. Did I really just say that? Redonkaballs? Huh, yup, guess I did. I was showing my crazy today. I digress… mom would tell me she never liked him because that's what moms did. And then she'd hug me and tell me to come over as if we didn't see each other just yesterday. Or she'd show up on my doorstep with a fresh baked good item. Wait a minute… a fresh baked good? Why did I think that it was a bad idea to call mom again? I quickly shot her a text to let her know, that way I didn't have to hear the sympathy that would inevitably make me start crying…again.

I thought about the things he said… that all it seemed like I wanted to do was work and read. That I didn't want to do anything. He made it seem like I had no goals in life or anything. Did I have goals? Well, hell yeah, of course I did. I mean, I worked full time while I got my Bachelors and my Masters degrees. That shows drive. Those were goals. There was that 5K I ran a few years ago…that was a goal I set for myself, and I totally nailed it. I mentally high-fived myself until I realized that each of those things were past tense. Now I did a mental forehead slap. GAH!

When was the last time I'd picked something to achieve, planned for it, worked for it and earned it? Sheesh, I can't remember, it's been a while.

Craig and I had been together for three years, we met when he saw me running as I was getting ready for the first 5K I ran. I still can't figure out why he stopped to chat with me, considering I had stopped for a water break and was chugging water as a dying man gasps his last breath. I mean, I was not cute when I run. You've see those ads where gorgeously svelte women are running like gazelles, their long, brunette ponytails swaying gracefully back and forth, not a bead of sweat on them and breathing evenly? Yeah – so not me. You've heard of the ugly cry? I mastered the art of the ugly run…red faced, snot flying (ew, sorry), hair all frizzed up and nasty. Oh, and I sweat. A. Lot. So I guessed that I would never understand what he saw in me that day, what made him stop me and say hi.

It was kind of hard to believe that we've been together for three years, considering we didn't live together or anything. Any of my friends who had been together for even a year…hell, three months, were living together already. I wondered if that was a sign that we (and by 'we' I really mean 'he') wasn't really ever going to commit to a permanent relationship. But what had I set my mind on since then? I honestly didn't even create a mental goal of pushing that boy to the alter in the oh-so-subtle ways that women have honed for centuries. Would I marry him if he asked? Hell, YEAH! In a heartbeat. Did I ever let him know in any way… oops, maybe not.

I tried to think of anything 'big' we had done together, and I couldn't find anything. I had always just said we were a couple of old 'homebodies'. We never went on frivolous trips, did any outrageous, expensive nights out. I mean, I mentally had a hard time paying someone for the privilege of sleeping in their bed that thousands, if not millions, of people had slept in before. I mean, seriously? Was I the only one who thought that it was a little gross to possibly be sharing body dirt with millions of strangers? I watched that documentary, hell, we watched it together and I thought we were in agreement that it was the nastiest of nasties. Going out to 'fancy eatin' places' never really held much interest to me, because I was a fairly good cook (thanks to my mom) and I didn't see the point in spending thirty dollars or more on something I could do myself.

What I think that I was trying to say, is that in three years, we really hadn't done anything. Not. A. Damn. Thing. Looking back, I realized that he had tried. He had suggested a trip to Disney. I said that there would be too many kids so we wouldn't be able to see anything or enjoy the rides. He had wanted to go to Hawaii, I said it was too expensive and I really couldn't take the time off of work. He had tried. I hadn't.

I think it might be time to shake things up a bit…not because a man told me to, hell no. But because I think, maybe, possibly I'd gotten a little…well… boring.

I realized quickly that I was getting waaaaay too introspective, and a lot too self-centered. Seriously, have you seen how many times I've said 'I'? Holy crap on a stick! I thought it may be a good idea for me to get some therapy. I picked up my phone and call my bestie, Alex. It went to voicemail as always, so I hung up. I knew the drill. Three seconds later and my phone started playing 'The Bitch is Back'. That was the type of thing that happened when one was stupid enough to leave their phone unattended with their best friend… a new ringtone was added and assigned.

"Hey girl, what's up?" Alex chirped, always energetic to the point where you wondered if she used Red Bull as a chaser to five espressos.

"Uh… well…" I realized that I didn't think far enough in advance as to how I was going to get this out without sobbing. I decided to speed through it, "CraigJustLeftHere… IThinkHeBrokeUpWithMe… ButMaybeNot…"

"Okay, so you need some therapy?"

"Yes, I do…STAT"

"I'm on it, we'll be there in an hour and a half."

I heard the phone beep, and then it went dead. She didn't say goodbye, she didn't have to. I knew that in about two hours, I'd probably already be a bit tipsy, and my close circle of girls would be dishing out advice as quickly as a fast food restaurant dishes out heart attacks. I looked around the house and I realized that it looked a bit messy. I was perhaps a little obsessive when it came to neatness. I couldn't have the girls feel as if I'd fallen upon slovenliness since being tossed aside like a pair of soiled undies. So I spent the next hour and a half dusting, vacuuming, doing laundry and getting ready for the onslaught.

As expected, one and a half hours later, my front door burst open and the three women who were my strength burst through and encase me in a huge group hug. I was smooshed against Leah's boobs, but it was okay. They were big and squishy so it wasn't like it was uncomfortable…just…awkward.

I saw that Karyn had a telltale brown paper bag, and a plastic bag. I raised my eyebrows hopefully. "Cabernet Sauvignon and Chocolate Chip Cookie dough?"

"You know it, woman…so let's get you drunk and sugared up so you can tell us what that rat bastard did to you."

Two bottles later, I was feeling a bit…okay, a LOT tipsy, and the girls were telling me that Craig was an ass for walking out on me for something as silly as a book.

"It's not like he caught you with another man. Or like you swore off sex with him in favor of your vibrator." That was Alex… explains the ringtone, no?

My head was feeling a little fuzzy, so I took a second to form my words. Yeah, definitely a LOT tipsy. "Guys, the thing is, maybe he's right. I mean, we don't go anywhere…we don't DO anything…and I think it actually may be kinda my fault."

"So wait, he wanted to do stuff and you said no?" Karyn asked incredulously.

"Um, sorta."

"Explain, please. Don't make us beg you." That was Leah. She's usually really chill and sweet. But get three glasses into her and this was the result. Evil, slightly crazy Leah.

"So, he was always wanting to go take me to fancy restaurants, and I said no, because I don't see why we should pay so much money for food I can make just as well on my own. He wanted us to take a trip to Hawaii once a year or so ago, but it was so expensive, and I'm trying to stay in my boss' good graces, so I said we really couldn't."

I looked around the living room to a bunch of bugged out eyes and dropped jaws. Gulp. Yeah, I guess it really is on me that this might be over.

"So, if you all are broken up, that means he's single and fair game, right?"

"ALEX! You do NOT poach your best friend's ex-boyfriend… that is NOT cool." Mentally thanked Leah as my chin raised up a notch and I gave Alex the side eye.

"What? If he wants to take me to Hawaii, I wouldn't say no, no matter what the cost."

"Girls, girls, she's right. I effed up. So, what do I do about it? I think I'm in some sort of a rut, and I just don't know how to get out. We became, well, comfortable."

Groans went around the room. Leah was moaning, "That is the kiss of death of a relationship. Lord, you might has well have said he had a cute dick."

We all got crazy quiet staring at Leah. You see, she was the good one of all of us, and suddenly she developed sailor mouth. I started grinning, then chuckling, and then full on laughing. Everyone joined in and the hysteria raised about ten notches when Karyn snorted…and red wine flew out of her nose. Oh man, I lost it then. Lost. It.

"Oh ma Gawd it buuuuurns, it burns!" she complained, as she ran to the kitchen for a paper towel to wipe herself off.

Once we all calmed down (talk about several deep cleansing breaths), I announced to the group, "Okay, I'm in a rut, I need out. I need to get a life… I've become so boring I put myself to sleep…so, what do I do?"

"Sleep with his best friend."

"Get a make-over."

"Buy a new purse."

"Sleep with his dad."

We all turned and looked at Leah. Karyn walked over and snatched her wine glass away and said, "You're cut off." Leah tried to reach for her wine glass and fell off the couch, getting wedged between the couch and coffee table. We all burst into peals of laughter once again. I got up and ran to the bathroom, because I was pretty sure I was going to pee myself laughing on this one. Once we calmed down, Leah was back up on the couch with her arms crossed, and was glaring at us indignantly. "I think his dad is freaking hot."

"Okay, okay" I was trying to restore order to this 'meeting'. "Yes, Craig's dad is wicked hot. BUT…that's out of the question, and kind of incestuous since I was considered part of the family. I need a REAL course of action."

It got so quiet around the room as they tried to focus their buzzed minds on the topic at hand.

"Have you ever thought of taking some classes to learn a skill? I got something in the mail from that tech school. Like, they teach basket weaving and shit? What about trying something like that?" Karyn suggested.

"Why not set a goal for yourself, something to work towards?" Alex contributed.

"Hmmmmmm. Those aren't bad ideas. Let's start with the classes." I pulled out my laptop and Googled 'tech schools near Wareham, MA.' "Hey guys, looks like Cape Regional Tech has some. This must be the one you were talking about, Alex. That school isn't too far from here."

We all gathered around and looked at the class offerings. Feng Shui, Watercolors, Know Your Sewing Machine, Get Debt Free, Blogging for Beginners.

"Well, I could try the blog thingy," I said cautiously. "That would be a definite step outside my box. I couldn't even commit to a diary when I was ten, and when I tried, it was a pathetic attempt to make a world that didn't exist or make myself look cooler than I ever was."

I was still thinking about it when Alex grabbed my laptop and started tapping at the keys at a frantic pace. She sat back, gave me a huge grin and said, "You start Monday at 6:30pm."

"WHAT? You enrolled me already?"

"Hellz yeah, didn't want to give you a chance to back out. So the one thing you have to do as a perquisite or homework or whatever the hell you call it for this type of class is to come up with a blog topic."

Shit. I could barely choose which pair of undies to wear in the morning, or what color socks I wanted to wear. If I made it out of the house with matching socks it was a bonus.

"I wouldn't even begin to know what to write about. I mean, what do I have to add that might be interesting for someone to read? I couldn't even keep the supposed love of my life interested."

"Well, this is supposed to be about stepping outside your comfort zone, right? So maybe a blog about trying new things?" Karyn added quietly.

I looked at her and thought about it, tilting my head a little as I considered it. "You know, that's not a bad idea."

"Trying something new every day." Alex was trying out the topic idea. She nodded. "Yeah, that's a good idea."

"Every day?" I squeaked out. "How about every week? One new experience every week. Because every day is a bit overwhelming for me."

"Ohhhhhkaaaaayyyy, one a week." Alex drawled out. "BUT, we get to pick the things. OMG this will be awesome!" She was clapping her hands and bouncing up and down like an idiot. I wanted to go smack her upside the head a bit, but I'm a tiny bit scared of her so I stayed put. "Ashley, if it were up to you, you would try a new type of seasoning or some boring shit like that. You need to get out and experience life. Get a life. We will help – but you've got to trust us. Leah, Karyn…we'll all come up with some things for her to experience, and we'll take turns on choosing for the week. Ash, we will send you your topic on Monday, and you'll have until the following Sunday night to complete it and write about it for the class."

"Nothing illegal, guys, please." I noticed my hands started sweating and I was feeling a bit queasy. I felt my stomach turn and I launched myself towards the bathroom. After I relieved myself of copious amounts of wine and ice cream I returned to a living room that was suspiciously quiet. Hushed whispers flew back and forth between my soon to be former friends.

Oh, shit. I was screwed.

Chapter 2

Monday came and I found myself trudging to my blogging class as if I was anticipating entering an interrogation room. I couldn't tell you why I was so anxious to do this, but it really had me almost hyperventilating with nerves. STOP IT, I coached myself. You can do this, it's not for credit and it doesn't affect your career. Now pull on your big girl panties and walk on in there like a boss. I blew out a puff of air which moved my bangs into my eyes. Awesome. Now my eyes were all watery as the feeling of little needle burned them. In a frustrated motion I swiped my bangs back in place as I marched into the room and fell into one of the closest seats.

In rushed a young guy, maybe late twenties/early thirties, with dark hair. He had his head down so I figured he was just another adult seeking enrichment. I was surprised when he dropped his backpack on the instructor's desk, turning to face us while running his hands through his hair in a frazzled attempt to compose himself. He looked around the room, and when his eyes met mine I felt a jolt that went through my head to my toes. Holy blue eyes. OMG I internally swooned. I had a thing for clear blue eyes. Well, and a nice tight butt. I was easy to please that way. Dark hair and light blue eyes were a lethal combination for me. A little drool formed in the corner of my mouth. I unconsciously lifted my right hand to wipe it away, and realized he was still watching me. His eyes crinkled with humor and his lips lifted in a smirk. Oh man, I was done. Eye crinkles needed to be added to my list of swoon-worthy features. I knew who I would be thinking of tonight when I freshened up my batteries.

Whoa... I mentally shook myself. What was I thinking? I was still in a relationship, it was just on hiatus or sabbatical or whatever the hell we're calling it. No sleeping with teacher. I felt as if I got caught doing something wrong, and that I should be marched up to the white board in the front of the room and write 'I shall not fantasize about teacher while playing with B.O.B.' one hundred times on the white board. I took a long swig from my bottled water, the cold water would have to do until a cold shower was available. I mentally shook myself again, must not think of shower and teacher in the same thought sequence. Geez, what was wrong with me? It wasn't like it had been that long. Had it? I started to mentally count how long it had been and found myself growing a bit sheepish. No wonder I was singleish now.

I refocused my attention to Blue, who was starting his introduction. Apparently his name was Mark...hmmmm, Mark.... Oh Mark, I could do things with you that were illegal in thirteen states. GAH! What on earth was happening to me?

I started listening as he explained the purpose of the class.

"Okay, so you all are here for your own reasons. Maybe you wanted to make new friends. Maybe you think you have some point of view on something that you think people will actually give a damn about. Maybe you're just bored. I don't know and I'm not going to ask you what they are. But I'm going to help you set up a blog online, and set guidelines to complete the class. You are required to complete one blog post a week. You are also required to read each other's blogs. We will discuss them weekly, I want constructive criticism. The blogs will be kept anonymous, though, so please keep your names out of it. You were told that you had to come to this class with a blog idea. I'm going to ask that you write your blog idea, your blog name and the concept down, as well as your name and I'll collect that from you. Today you will be setting up your blog space, logging in, finding out how to maneuver around the space, add your content, add photos, change formats, etc. For next class, you'll need to do an intro blog. In your intro, I want you to explain what your blog will be about, what the journey will be. Again, please keep it anonymous for now. At the end of our six weeks together, we will reveal who wrote what, and discuss our experiences in the journey of maintaining their blog, and the interaction with anyone who read it. I do ask that you let your friends and family know about it as you feel comfortable, because you SHOULD have readers. Any questions? No? Okay, so start writing down your blog titles, concepts and names. I'll come around and grab them."

Um, so okay, this was the point where I should let you know I did NOT think about my blog in advance. I knew I was supposed to, but let's face it, my friends picked out my blog concept for me. A new experience every week. I grabbed a piece of paper and as my pen hit the paper my brain went blank for a moment. Then I just went for it.

Name: Ashley MacKillop

Blog title: Singleish

Concept: My boyfriend sort of broke up with me but not really. I'm in a rut and a half where I don't do anything interesting or fun anymore so after a drunk night of wine and ice cream fueled introspection, my best friends signed me up for this class and they will be forcing me to do one new thing every week. The kicker is, they get to choose my adventure each week and I get no choice in the matter. I'm terrified at what they are going to choose and I'm doing my best to be extra nice to each of them so it's nothing particularly crazy.

Well, that was honest, at least. He was probably going to think that I was psychotic. But I didn't care what he thought about me and my choice of topic...or friends. It should be interesting, to say the least. I just hope that I haven't done anything I've forgotten about to Alex, Leah and Karyn that they would be paying me back for. Karma is a bitch and so are my girls when they'd been drinking. I hoped that these topics are chosen sober.

We go over setting up the blog, I chose a pink, florally girlie pattern for mine, and set up our log-in information. Class is dismissed with a reminder to write an intro post explaining the blog, sort of like the concept paragraph we wrote up for Mark by the next time we meet, next Monday.

Leaving the room we had to walk past Mark, who was being careful to say goodbye to everyone, make eye contact and wishing us the best. When I was next in line, he shook my hand, mumbled a 'good luck' and did not look me in the eyes. I was confused as I said, "Uh, thanks?" and walked out the door in a dumb stupor. WTF was that? Everyone got a heartfelt thought but me? Geez, as if I wasn't feeling vulnerable and tore open enough, the hot teacher that I would be having inappropriate fantasies about tonight couldn't even look me in the eye. Did I look that hideous today? Coyote ugly? Without thinking, I gnawed at my arm a bit in a coyote ugly motion my dad and I would have done together, but Daddy wasn't there to appreciate the gesture, so instead I looked like a freak. A bit.

Once I got home, I poured my glass of red liquid courage, and opened up the laptop I stored under my couch. I opened up my new blog and as my fingers hovered over the keyboard I paused, how much was I willing to share? How 'real' was I willing to be in my posts? I tilted my head and thought, go big or go home. Let's do this bitch.

After taking a long swallow of my wine, I started typing.

"This is not my idea. This is something I'm doing because I was told that I'm pretty much a boring excuse for a human being. I was told this by a person I trusted my heart to. I loved him and I would have married him, but now I can't because he put our relationship on a hiatus. We are now a sitcom on break for the summer or winter. We are not an 'us' until he decides that I am no longer lacking in ambition and goals. The break started because I ignored my boyfriend of three years unintentionally, but that was the straw that broke the camel's back. He walked away because he tried to create moments with me and have adventures with me when I was not interested. I turned my back. I said no. This is what made him slam on the breaks and say he needed a chance to think about things. It takes two to tango, and he was dancing alone. I thought we were happy homebodies, but I realize I wasn't paying much attention to him. I was more interested in reading then playing out my own adventures with my real, living, breathing Prince Charming. Do we find each other in the end of this journey? Who knows? But I think it's time for me to find myself in the journey. My best friends and I met up and after consuming enough wine to intoxicate a small village in Madagascar, devised this plan to take a class on blogging to get me out of my rut. Seemed like a brilliant idea at the time. My friends will be choosing my 'try something new each week' adventure. I won't know what it is until I get the email or text. I promise to be honest in my reaction and my execution. Not knowing what it is they have planned for me, this may be NSFW. I'm just hoping I haven't pissed them off in a past life or something. So as I find out, you find out. I will be truthful in my experiences in carrying out their planned 'adventures'...so help me God."

With that I dutifully hit save and sent our instructor a message to the email he shared with us letting him know I'd completed the assignment. I had always enjoyed being the top of the class in undergrad, so I guess I was back in that place of being the top of the class. (Oh, and for those of you keeping score, yes, I also have a graduate degree, but that was so effing hard that I honestly only cared about finishing without having to repeat any courses. So I was proud to be able to say I passed, but I imagined that I'd ended up somewhere around the lower end of the totem pole). Mark had suggested we create a 'dummy' email address for our blog, so that our personal email account didn't get bogged down with whatever was sent our way once the blog was made public. I didn't think that there was going to be a line of eligible bachelors knocking at my proverbial virtual wall after I hit 'submit', but I did what he suggested, anyway. I.Am.Singleish@gmail.com.

I remembered he told us that we should encourage friends and family to read our 'blog', if for no other reason than to get honest feedback from it. I thought it would be a better idea to leave family out and just allow the three co-conspirators to have access. My mom might be scandalized to read whatever it is these three musketeers come up with for me to do. I'm pretty sure my dad still saw me as the four year old who was terrified of the blue haired clown they got me for my birthday. In my defense, blue hair is not naturally occurring, and therefore was incredibly freakish. My siblings – well – I'd always be their kid sister and that might be weird for them and for me. Mostly for me. Don't get me started on the nieces. So best friends-slash-co-conspirators in the horror that was my life were the only ones to get access. Those bitches better read it religiously and be nice. Or they wouldn't want to know what I'd be doctoring their next meal with.

Chapter 3

It was crazy busy at work during the week, so busy I managed to forget about the crazy of my personal life (or lack thereof). Before I knew it, I was standing in front of the classroom door ready to start week two of being a blogster. Or bloginator. I think I liked bloginator better...

Mark walked in and I sat up a little straighter, pen in hand and at the ready to take whatever nuggets of blog perfection he was to toss our way. Yeah, that sounded wicked sarcastic in my mind, too.

"Alright everyone, I was able to go through everyone's blogs last week, and was thrilled to see that not only did you all take the assignment seriously, you also all set up the dummy email addresses that I suggested. I sent my comments to that email address, so if you were really on top of your game, you already know what my thoughts were." He smiled at the lot of us, mirth apparent in his eyes as he saw more than half of his class nonchalantly reaching for their cell phones. I won't lie, I was one of them. I just wanted to know if he thought I was as much of a freak of nature as I felt when I was writing my intro post.

I quickly logged in and was shocked that I had four emails. I found his quickly and read it, a blush creeping from my neck to my forehead as I read his words.

"I have never laughed so much reading an intro post as I did yours. If you were to continue this style forever, I have a feeling you will have followers. Keep it up, keep it snarky, and I can not wait to hear what your friends have planned for you. Oh, and maybe once this class is done and it's not unethical, we could have drinks sometime. As friends."

Holy shit, he wants to take me out on a date? I looked up briefly and saw him looking my way with a knowing smirk on his face. Why is it that I find smirks sexy? WHY? I looked back down and re-read the last line. As friends. Great. So now I didn't know whether I'm in a relationship or not, nor do I know if I was asked on a date or not. It was so much easier when life was uncomplicated and I knew where I stood. Except, I guess I didn't. GRRRR!

I saw that the next email down was labeled 'mission impossible' and it was courtesy of Karyn. I guess she drew the first straw for my blog assignment. I opened it up so that I knew what I was facing this week.

"Your mission, if you choose to accept it...except you have to accept it mwa ha ha ha is to... get a pet. And not a goldfish or a parakeet. You have to get something that will require you to care for it, and that will potentially bring a little messiness and a lot of happiness into your singleish life. Please don't kill me...or the pet!"

SONOFABITCH! Twenty heads swiveled to stare at me all slack-jawed. I think I might have said that out loud. Oops... I slid down in my seat and stared at my blank piece of paper as if it was the most fascinating thing in the universe. A pet? I had to get a pet? I always had pets as a kid, but never thought of it as an adult. I liked things neat. Pets were NOT neat.

"Okay, well, now we know how Ashley feels about this, but yes, I expect you to all check in to all your classmate's blogs during the week and leave constructive comments." He started handing out sheets of paper with blog sites on them, but as he promised, no names. I scanned the topics, auto repair, making your own cleaning products, abstaining from sex, beer making... and singleish. "When you type your blogs, please pay attention to spelling, grammar and tense. I know that may not seem like a big deal, but in the intro posts I saw people going from past to present so much, that I got whiplash trying to keep up."

A few people chuckled at his weak attempt at humor. Such a shame, to be that good looking and have a weak sense of humor. Then again, blogging is not exactly a titillating subject matter. I started to feel myself go warm. Mentally adding titillating to my ever growing list of words I couldn't think of in the same context as Mark. I didn't need to think of him anywhere near my ti...was it getting warm in here or was it just me? I started to fluff the front of my shirt, trying to cool myself down. No one else seemed warm. Great, just me.

As I was walking out of the class I felt a warm hand on my arm. "Ashley, could I have a moment?"

When I turned around, I was met with two bright blue eyes that I had no business being so close to in my current state. Gulp.

"Uh, sure, Mark. What's up?" What's up? Is that really what I could come up with? Smooth, Ash...real smooth.

"I wanted to make sure you had no problems with the assignments. You seemed a bit upset when I was talking about the requirements to read other blogs." I gave him a confused look at first. I didn't remember being upset about the assignments he handed out, only the one my soon-to-be-former friend handed out. Oh no, he was referring to my little outburst. How embarrassing. I started laughing at the absurdity of it all, and he was giving me the look that said "is it time for the straight jacket, or too soon?"

"Oh my God, Mark, no… it wasn't that at all. I had just opened up my first 'task' from one of my friends for my blog. Sorry I shouted a bit during class, but needless to say, it was NOT what I expected."

A look of relief and understanding filled his eyes. "What on earth are they having you do if it got that type of reaction?"

"Oh, no. No way! You're just going to have to wait for it, like the rest of the class." I gave him my sauciest smile possible, turned and sashayed out of the room. Yes, I sashayed, my hips were trying to be hypnotizing. Don't judge me.

Now I had to get a pet, and not a goldfish or a parakeet. They knew me too well to know I would have gone for the goldfish. I mean, they tend to be more decorative than anything else. I allowed myself a few moments to fantasize about a decorative fish tank that would work beautifully in my living room, allowing me my neat freakiness while still complying with the task at hand. Sigh.

I was still pondering this dilemma while sitting in my living room. I realized that whatever I chose had to be something that would fit my work schedule, and because I was living alone, the critter had to be able to be alone for a bunch of hours during the day. So clearly, not a dog. I guessed that I might as well give into the stereotype of being a single woman with a cat. Just great. I had now become a caricature of a spinster. Alone, lonely with a house full of cats. I should get a new housecoat too, while I was at it. If I was going to go all crazy cat lady, I should go big or go home.

By the next morning, I had resigned myself to my spinsterhood, and was trying to decide how to go about procuring a cat. I could check the classifieds online, see if anyone on Facebook happens to have a cat they are relieving themselves of, or check out an animal shelter. Hmm, I kind of liked that idea. An animal shelter. That way I would not only accomplish this ridiculous task, I would also make the world a better place for it. I briefly pictured myself atop a mountain, wind blowing, my superhero cape billowing out behind me. In the background you would hear a deep announcer's voice: "A lone woman…terminally lone…saves the world from animal homelessness one abandoned cat at a time."

I made a list of everything I would need to keep a cat alive. Litter box, litter, food bowls, a couple toys, some cat kibble (is that what it's called?). I figured that I would go shopping at lunch tomorrow and then swing by the local shelter on my way home. No sense in delaying the inevitable.

***

When I walked into the shelter's cat room, I was overwhelmed. So many different cats to choose from, so many color options and sizes. I don't know what I was anticipating, but this was NOT it. There were well over thirty cats who were begging to be released from their tiny jails. How in the hell was I supposed to pick just one? Wait a minute, who said I had to pick just one? I was a spinster, we should have more than one…maybe like two, or three or ten.

Feeling much more confident in my cat adoption tactics, I marched out to the front desk and said "I'm here to adopt a cat, or two, or five. Hell, I want to adopt an entire armful of cats!"

Have you ever had one of those moments where what you were about to say sounded so awesome in your head, but was an epic fail when it actually came out of your mouth? Apparently, when you declared that you are looking to adopt an armful of cats they suspected that you were an escapee of a mental institution, or that you were a member of some cult that was looking for a form of sacrifice.

"Uh, okay, Ma'am," stuttered the volunteer behind the desk, "We, um, have an application you have to fill out first, and then you have to be interviewed by the Director."

Wait, what? An interview? I didn't think it was going to be so hard to get a cat. I wasn't prepared, I didn't bring my resume or list of personal references. WTF?

So I sat down with my questionnaire and started filling it out. When I get to "Reason you would like to adopt the pet" I paused for a moment and thought "oh hell, why not".

"My boyfriend of three years decided I was so boring that I was putting him in to a monotony derived coma. He walked out on me, but apparently we might still be together. But I doubt it. So I'm single. And female. And any good, self-respecting, terminally single female must. have. cats. I'm embracing my apparent terminal

singledom, and therefor would like to adopt a bunch of cats. Now, please."

I mentally patted myself on the back for being honest in my answering of the form. Surely that sweet little volunteer would understand the predicament I have found myself in. I turned in the adoption application and watched as she read over my answers. I saw her eyes widen in surprise, I figured that she must have been so impressed with my honesty. This was going to be easy, I was getting my cats today.

Sometimes, I was forced to realize that I had an extreme inability to read people. Honesty was clearly not the best policy in this case. A frightening, somewhat militant looking woman came marching around the corner, with my carefully written application gripped in her fist.

"Is this some type of joke? You want to adopt a 'bunch of cats' because you got dumped?" I shrank back a bit, I mean, when you put it that way it seemed less heroic and a little more, I don't know, crazy.

"Ma'am, yes, ma'am" I said before I could stop myself. General Kitty Litter (yes, I gave her a name) turned from a light pink in color to a somewhat lobsterish shade of red. I thought that maybe I was not getting my cats today.

"These animals have been abandoned for reasons that your self-absorbed mind couldn't possibly begin to comprehend. Cats get turned in because they meow too much. Some don't meow enough. One was turned in because he didn't match the furniture. One seventeen year old cat was turned in because the owners were retiring and wanted to travel. Therefore, I have to be certain that whomever I adopt these lives to plans on keeping them forever. This is a LIFE we are talking about, not an accessory or a pint of ice cream meant to make the boo-boo go away that the mean man left on your heart. You will not be adopting from this shelter. Please. Leave. Now."

I was shocked, both at the intense level of venom that was sent my way from the General, but also that these animals were turned in for such stupid reasons. I mean, I guess I just had always thought there must be something a little wrong with an animal that gets turned in. When I looked around the lobby I realize that there were about ten people staring at me, some with pity, and some with contempt. I hung my head in a mixture of embarrassment and shame and slunk out the side exit. I had just stepped out the door when I heard someone running to approach me.

"Excuse me, miss?" I turned to see who was talking to me. The woman staring back looked sad, as if she had lost her best friend. I immediately felt bad for her, but didn't know why. "I heard the Director, um, talking to you in the lobby, and if you are really wanting a cat, I have one. I mean, I was here to surrender her, anyway, and this way she wouldn't have to live in kitty prison."

"Really, you'd give me your cat?" I realized that I was acting way too enthusiastically, so I toned it down a bit. "Why? What's wrong with her?"

"N-nothing is wrong with her. She's very sweet, super friendly. I just have to move and I can't take her with me. No one would take her, so I had no other choice, I had to bring her here. She's in my car if you'd like to meet her."

I found myself walking to the woman's car, and peering in to a small cat carrier. Looking back at me was a pair of terrified green eyes. This kitty had a black face surrounded by bright, white whiskers. I felt the cat's fear and knew that I would not be letting this one get into the shelter. Maybe I wasn't allowed to adopt from them, but I could at least help reduce the number of animals inside by keeping one out.

"Uh, is she healthy?" I couldn't think of what the right questions were.

"Yeah, super healthy, only two years old. I have her shot records and everything from the vet, so you don't have to worry about all that right now." Right, the vet. I have to get a vet. I guess I could just take her to the same doctor she's been seeing. "Will you take her? Please?"

"Okay, I don't have a carrier for her, though. I figured that I'd adopt and get one of those cardboard thingies they give you."

"Oh, you can have her carrier, her blanket, her toys and leftover food. I'm just so glad I was able to find someone nice to take her."

"Um, okay…" Something seemed off. I mean, if she heard the reason I was all but kicked out of the shelter, she shouldn't think I was a super nice person. Oh well, I shook that thought out and took the kitty from her owner. "Oh, what's her name?"

"Penny. She's a black and white tuxedo cat that my kids thought looked like a penguin. We couldn't name her Penguin because that's not a very girly name, so we came up with Penny."

I thought Penny was as good a name as any, so I took Penny and set her up in the front seat of my car.

"Hi, Penny, I guess I'm your new mom. I haven't had a cat since I was about six years old, but I didn't do much but pet and play with old Gunny. So, this is kind of a new experience for both of us."

Big green eyes peered out at me from the carrier. "Mrowl" she chirped.

Huh, if I didn't know any better, I'd swear that cat understood me and was answering me. It had already started. I was becoming the crazy cat lady. Pretty soon all you would see on my Facebook wall was pictures of my cat and stories of her antics. I figured I might as well get a start on it, whipped out my phone and took a picture. With the darkness of the carrier and her face being black, it actually looked like a cool photo with glowing green eyes and bright white whiskers.

I posted her photo up on Facebook, *"Look who has her crazy cat lady starter kit!"* and headed home.

Once Penny and I got home, I kept her in the car for a little bit so that I could get her litter box set up. I had read online that you should get your cat's litter pan situated, and let her see that first. Wham...litter trained kitty. I put all of her stuff in the house so that it wasn't too messy, grabbed her carrier and took her on the grand tour. I found myself talking to her, which seemed like a crazy thing to do, but she 'mrowled' back at me, so again, I was pretty sure she caught on to everything I was saying to her. We got up to my room and I set the carrier on the bed and opened the door.

She finally crawled out of the carrier and I was shocked. My sweet little girl was not so...little. She was downright obese. Holy crap on a stick, she must have ate that poor woman out of house and home. That had to be the reason she gave her up. "Well, my pleasantly plump baby girl" I said to her in a sing-song voice, "First order of business is some low fat cat chow and plenty of exercise." Upon that proclamation, she hoisted her hind leg up, gave me the best possible feline eff you look she could give and proceeded to give her rear end a thorough washing. While I had to appreciate her flexibility, I mean, she could reach parts of herself that I couldn't reach on myself; I couldn't help but feel as if I'd been somewhat dismissed.

I was in the process of changing into my yoga pants and t-shirt, and putting my clothes in the laundry and my trusty navy blue pumps in the closet. I wasn't going to win any awards for sexiness or sassiness with those shoes, but they were comfortable, sensible, and went with almost everything I wore. When I came back from the laundry, Penny was no longer on the bed. I looked under the bed, in the bathroom and was getting worried until I looked in my closet and saw her in amongst my shoes. She was giving herself a bath. I was thrilled, because I had read online that was a sign that they were comfortable. Actually, a lot of peoples' cats seem to hide under the bed or dresser the first few days, so I figured this meant Penny and I were kindred spirits meant to be together. Two terminally single women united against the world. Wow, she was really going to town on her attempts at cleanliness, I bet her hind and tail were going to sparkle once she finished. Hey, I respected her, she must be a neatnic like me.

I heard my doorbell and scurried downstairs. Who was at the door but my three alleged best friends. They had a bottle or two (okay, three) of wine, so I let them in, despite being pretty peeved at them. I heard some pretty intense meowing from upstairs. "Good girl", I thought, you reject their presence now, too. But she calmed down so I thought maybe it just had to do with the new environment and not really knowing where she was.

"Where is it?" That would be Karyn. She who was at the top of my kill list.

"What in the hell were you thinking, having me get a pet? Do you even know what I've been through today?" I launched into an explanation of my time in the shelter and the shady woman in the parking lot. Leah had to excuse herself a couple times to use the bathroom from laughing so hard. Okay, okay, I get it, it's a funny story. But have you ever noticed that funny stories are funnier when they don't happen to you?

I heard another batch of meows from upstairs. I frowned as I looked up in the direction of the bathroom. I mean, I didn't want her to be scared in her new house, especially with the appearance of the three shrews. I shook my head, she'd be fine. She's a cat…they are known for their independence and not needing anyone. Sure enough, the mewling stopped, and all was quiet again. Well, except for my friends.

The girls looked at each other and let out a collective 'awwwwwww' after having heard Penny's quiet cry.

"Fine, if you would like to go meet Penny, she was in my closet last I saw. Oh, and she's a little bit plus size. But please don't say anything about, I think she's a little sensitive about her size."

After giving me a few incredulous looks, the girls charged up the stairs to meet my furry family member.

I set to opening a bottle of wine, when I heard a loud shriek from upstairs. I set the bottle down and scrambled up the stairs, worried that something was wrong with my cat. I mean, seriously, what type of crazy cat lady was I turning out to be if my first cat got sick or injured within its first twelve hours with me?

When I walked in all three of the girls where on the knees, peering in to my closet. I heard them murmur "oh, you good girl" and "what a sweet momma".

Wait…Momma? Sweet Momma?

I pushed into the fray and in my closet, on my favorite pair of comfortable, sensible navy pumps, my new cat Penny lay with three, wriggling bodies, lots of soft mewling filling the air.

Now I felt like a complete ass for telling her she was fat. The poor thing was pregnant. Hm, I guess that was what was wrong with her. I started laughing, softly at first but quickly it turned into hysterics, gulping air and falling over on my side. My friends looked at me as if I'd lost it. "You okay, Ash?" asked Alex.

"Oh…my…God… I said I wanted an armful of cats… I got what I asked for."

We all got a laugh out of that, and then Leah said, "I have to say, I give her bonus points for taking out those hideous shoes."

"What the hell are you talking about? I loved those shoes." I gagged internally as I looked at my navy pumps. Although they were my favorite shoes, they were no match for the newborn kitten birthing goo that covered them. Yeah, they were going to get tossed.

"Well, no one else did…"

"Everyone hated those shoes! There is not a soul out there who thought that there was a single redeeming quality about those nasty things. First of all…navy is NOT a cute color. But a square toe? A thick, clunky heal? Nuns at catholic school wear shoes with more sex appeal than those."

"MROWL"

Oops, I guess Penny didn't appreciate us yelling around her kittens. I take another look and see one orange kitten, one black kitten and one white, orange and black kitten. All three were rooting around their mom, and latching on to start feeding. I heard a loud, rusty purr and looked at my cat. Those green eyes that were filled with fear only hours ago now had a contented look about them. I couldn't help but feel as if she was thanking me for giving her a safe place to have her babies.

I felt a warm feeling growing inside of me. Was it indigestion? Was it love? I just know that this morning I lived alone, and now we were a family of five.

"Hey, congrats, Grandma." Karyn said excitedly. I glared at her. She was the reason this happened. I no longer had a warm and fuzzy feeling flowing through me. I smacked her on the arm.

"This is all your fault!"

Chapter 4

All in all, I thought I took the surprise of an extra three furries in stride. In my mind I was so cool calm and collected, but in reality I was taking about a hundred pictures of these freakishly adorable creatures and posting them on Facebook and on my blog. Finding new homes for them was so not an option. I'd already said I wanted and armful of cats, well, now I had them!

My girls, on the other hand, were completely losing their shit over the kittens. Okay, and the fact that Penny had given birth to them on top of the allegedly offensive shoes. Obviously, at about an hour old, their eyes and little ears were closed, and all they really gave a crap about was nursing their poor mom to a size zero. Yes, I was a little jealous of Penny's weight loss plan.

I thought a little about the living situation. I figured that Penny would probably want to keep her kittens close for a while, which means my current layout of food bowls, blankets and litter boxes would not work. I utilized the free labor I had on hand, hey, 'will work for alcohol', and set the girls to work moving my shoes and clothes to the guest room closet. I put Penny's litter box in the master bathroom, making sure she saw me put it in there. I would swear on a stack of Bibles that the cat slowly closed her eyes and nodded at me, as if saying "I see what you did, and I approve."

I put the food and water bowls just outside the closet door, so that the kittens couldn't accidentally get into them, and then her blankets went into the closet. "Mrowl!" she exclaimed, standing up to move over. Unfortunately one of the kittens was still attached to her nips…so watching that poor thing dangle a little and then finally let go and plop gently on the carpet made us all laugh. Penny gave us a proper cat eff you glare, turned with her tail ram-rod straight gave us a view of the all seeing eye as she stalked to the soft bed of blankets, starting to move a kitten on at a time to the new nest. She then apparently decided they'd gotten filthy since their last cleaning (what, an hour ago?) and started giving each of their faces a cleaning, one at a time.

The four of us grinned at each other like a pack of simpletons. It was just so freaking sweet, seeing her looking after her newborn babies. I was already in love with each and every one of them. I was picturing a home with kittens growing up and chasing each other around the house. Amazing how it made the house seem less big and empty. I guess I was just waiting for the pitter patter of kitty paws to fill up the quiet.

"Alright, ladies, I'd say it's time for us to toast the arrival of the fur balls." That would be Alex, had I mentioned yet how sentimental she gets? I hadn't? Good.

I bounced down the stairs to the kitchen to get the food put together. I was beyond happy about how this worked out. I was not anywhere close to telling Karyn that I loved what she'd forced me to do. This is seriously the most smiling that I've done in as long as I can remember.

Suddenly, I realized it had gotten really quiet in the living room. Inappropriately quiet. Silence is golden, except for when it relates to my girls…in that case, silence was a very, very bad thing. Next thing you know I hear the clomping of their feet on my stairs as they made a procession down my stairs to the living room. What the hell were these crazies up to this time?

"Burn! Burn! Burn!" I shook my head and looked as my now somewhat gooey prized pair of pumps were being carried down the stairs by Alex like a virgin sacrifice.

Alex carried the gak filled pumps to my brick fireplace, where Karyn and Leah had lit a roaring fire that rivaled that of an English manor. I knew what was coming, but it broke my spirit a little to see my favorite pair of shoes tossed into the burning flames. "Noooooooo!" I looked around to see who made that cry, and realized it was me. Was I really that attached to a pair of shoes? I watched, quietly, as they tossed my shoes into the fire and they burst into a bluish flame. I mentally sent up a prayer to whoever the God of beloved navy pumps was. They were good to me, be good to them.

Alex, Leah and Karyn were beyond giddy at the birth of the kittens and demise of my trusty shoes. They jabbered on all night long about how cute the babies were, what we should name them and who should take me shopping for replacement shoes.

"So, Grandma, what do you think the kittens should be named?" asked Leah snidely. Yup, she's got some wine in her again.

Jeez, names? I thought I'd gotten off the hook by getting a free cat that was two years old and knew her name.

"Uh, I dunno…the black one is black, which is dark. It's dark when it's midnight outside, so, that one can be Midnight?"

They gave me a look of, 'seriously, is that the best you can do?'

"So, I kinda rescued these kittens by taking in their mom. I mean, if I hadn't taken her, all four would be in an animal shelter tonight, right? Who knows what would have happened then. So for the orange one, I guess 'Rescue'…well, maybe 'Ressie'. Yeah, Ressie's a good name."

At this point Alex did a forehead slap. She very sarcastically said, "So what, the calico will be named Callie because she's a calico and that makes it oh-so-clever? I'm sure there aren't already a million calico cats named Callie."

Yes, I was going to suggest that the calico be named Callie. But now I had to think quickly. "No, crazy, I was going to name her Callie Berry, because she's too damned pretty to just be Callie."

"Mmmmhmmmmmmm" Alex raised an eyebrow while looking at me. She knew, I was totally going to take the easy road on naming all the kittens.

"Now that you have a cat, I mean, a cat and her kittens, what are you going to do next?" Leah asked. "I mean, your initial task was just for a pet, you now have four. Are you really going to keep them all?"

I thought back to the scared green eyes I saw peering back at me in the carrier. It wasn't Penny's fault that she was an unwed kitty mom, and I wasn't going to be the one to make her say goodbye to her kittens. I would, however, get her and the kittens 'fixed' so they couldn't have any more babies. It's bad enough that my friends were calling me 'Grandma'. Maybe as a part of my spinsterhood I could start the 'Ashley MacKillop Home for Unwed Cats' and help turn the lives of pregnant and single felines around. I would teach them life skills, help them learn a trade, how to make a living for themselves, keep them off of the cruel streets and out of a life of prostitution.

"I guess we're just going to play it by ear, and see how we get along. But, I can't see letting the kittens go. I mean, she gave birth to them, those are her children. How can I take them away from her now?"

A knowing look passed along the room.

***

Later that night, after the girls left, I grabbed my Kindle and cuddled up on the couch. But then, I don't know, I didn't feel right sitting downstairs while my new furry family was holed up in my closet. I grabbed my Kindle and a pillow from the couch and went upstairs to my bedroom. I put the pillow on the floor next to the closet and started reading. I looked into the closet every once in a while, melting a little bit more every time I saw Penny bathing her babies, or helping them nurse.

"You're a good momma, Pen," I murmured, reaching over to pet her on the head. I was rewarded with a deep rumbly purr that instantly made me relax more than any of the Scottish Lairds and Lasses of my historic romance novels did. "Yup, you did good, Momma girl."

We sat there, woman and cat, for what seemed like hours. I filled her in on everything that had been going on up to her arrival. Every once in a while she would reply with a "Mrowl!" or a wet purring noise. Somehow between petting her and hearing her purring, I fell asleep sitting up propped against the wall. When I woke up three hours later, my neck was stiff and my back was freaking killing me.

"Ughhhhh." I looked around for my cat, who it appears had the good sense to crawl into her bed while I was sleeping and was curled up with three tiny furry bodies. I looked at the clock, it was 2:00am. I realized I hadn't written about the day's adventures yet, so I stood up, stretched my back and neck a little...OW!...and padded downstairs to my laptop.

I thought about the day, seriously, how was I going to fit in everything that happened in a reasonable post? My fingers paused over the keyboard as I contemplated what to write, and then my fingers started flying.

"Crazy Cat Lady Collection Started. Get a pet, that's what the email said. Well, today I guess I did the 'go big or go home' version of that..."

When I looked at the clock again, it was now 3:30am, which means I had exactly an hour and a half to get some shut eye and be mentally ready for work. Maybe I should have waited until the weekend to embark on this particular adventure. I had to somehow drag myself through two days of work until I could sleep in during the weekend.

***

There's a wonderful thing about caffeine, the more you consume, the more you are able to function. Please note that I said 'function', not 'focus'. I consumed two cups of coffee at home when I woke up, swung by the coffee shop on the way to work and got a grande dark roast with a shot of espresso. At work I was sipping green tea from 9:00am till noon. I barely took any breaks at work, tearing through my workload like a mad woman on a mission. I finally took a moment to run to the bathroom (because of three coffees and a tanker truck full of green tea) and when I looked in the mirror I was shocked to see somewhat frizzy hair, pallid skin and wide, blood-shot eyes. I was frightening. No wonder everyone was steering a wide berth. Crap, I have to pull this together, and quickly. I splashed water on my face, then used my wet hands to moisten my hair, grabbing an ever available elastic from my purse and I pulled my hair into a tight bun. Then pinched some color into my cheeks to make my face look a little less corpsy. See, there is some good knowledge to be gained in reading historical romance novels.

I somehow made it through the day, but if you asked me what I had accomplished you'd get a blank stare and then 'blink, blink'. Yup, one of those days. During the day my desk looked like a paper explosion, but by the end of the day it was cleaned up, so I knew I did something between 9:00am and 6:00pm. Well, something besides coming close to having an overdose on caffeine.

As I got into the car I realized I had a text message from Craig from 6:00am. Huh, it seemed strange, but I hadn't been thinking of him and how much it hurt to have him walk away from us. I opened the message and read, *"Hey, Ash, sorry for the other night. Have to go out of state for work for a couple weeks. Will call you when I get back. –C."* Well, that didn't answer any questions. I growled as I hit the sleep button on my phone. I was so not going to deal with that right now. I had a momma cat at home that needed some love.

After I checked on the cats, freshening up Penny's water and food, scooping out her box (ew), I settled down on the sofa with a glass of wine.

When I opened up my laptop, I had a reminder I'd set to check my blog email. Opening up my i.am.singleish account I was shocked to find four emails. That meant four people had read about my feline adventure today. I did a mental happy dance, and imagined myself for a moment as a world class blogger. I would win all blogging awards. Baby bloggers would come to me, seeking my advice as if I was the oracle at Delphi. Imagining the wealth that would come with the associated fame, I opened the first email.

"Death to the nun shoes!"

Huh, maybe fame and fortune wasn't coming my way after all. I looked at the email addresses. Alex, Karyn, Leah and someone I didn't know.

I open the one I don't know, figuring I already know what type of comments I would get from the girls.

"Hi Ashley, it's Mark, your instructor from the Blog class. Anyway, congrats on your new cat and kittens. WOW... you're right. Go big or go home. Anyway, I have some toys that my cat, Charcoal, seems to deem unworthy, I thought your new little family might appreciate them. I'll bring them to class Monday night."

I sat back, surprised to hear from Mark. I would be lying if I said I wasn't a little interested in him, but I wasn't ready to act on it. I mean, I was in love with Craig, and I needed to know what's going on there. It felt unfinished and I have always been a loyal person. I'd never been the cheating type and I refused to start now. However, there was maybe a little teenager level crush going on, and I got wicked giggly thinking that teacher might be hot for me. I could at least indulge in some innocent fantasies. That never hurt anyone, right? I rested my head on the couch cushion, closed my eyes to imagine his sweet blue eyes, crinkled at the corner from smiling too much. He would have leaned towards me, closing his eyes as he tenderly brushed my lips with his. As he pulled away the image I had of him in my mind morphed into Craig, brown hair and warm brown eyes. I felt the palm of his hand cupping my cheek and I started to feel truly homesick for him. Sigh. I was hopeless. Couldn't even indulge in some not quite innocent fantasies about my instructor, without my maybe boyfriend, maybe ex-boyfriend barging in on them.

Chapter 5

Saturday came, finally, and with it came my trek to the coffee shop downtown to meet up with the girls for our weekly coffee. I know, it wasn't like we didn't see each other all the time anyway, but this was our chance to relax, unwind and just chew the fat a bit without the alcohol. Which meant, we remembered all of it the next day. I walked up to the table where Leah, Karyn and Alex were talking excitedly and animatedly. I wondered what was up, and in anticipation already had a smile growing on my face.

"Hey, ladies!" I slid into the booth next to Karyn.

"Oh, hey…" I got the most half-hearted greeting a human should ever have to endure. No one would look me in the eye, and suddenly they were looking at their cups of coffee, the stacks of creamer and the ceiling tiles as if they were the most important things on the planet. I couldn't figure out what had turned me into a pariah. I did a quick breath check, nope, that wasn't it. Reached up and patted my hair, seemed as if its unruly self was behaving today for once. Nope, had no idea why it was that my presence created a conversational cease fire.

"Um, is everything okay? Do I have something in my teeth? What's going on?"

"Nothing, everything's fine, Ash." I felt less than convinced with Alex's answer, especially since it still came without any form of eye contact.

"Seriously guys, you're freaking me out. What the hell is going on? You shut up as soon as I come near the table, and you all are never quiet. You won't look me in the eye. What. The. Hell?"

Yeah, I was pissed. I mean, this wasn't like them and I knew I hadn't done anything to upset anyone; well, I didn't think I had done anything.

They all glanced at each other, and then Karyn sighed. She brought her left hand on the table and what I saw was about one carat of princess cut brilliance staring back at me. I felt as if I'd been sucker punched in the stomach. She and Chris had been dating less than two years, and he knew he loved her enough to make it a forever type of thing. I guess I wasn't quite as lucky.

I shook off the selfish and jealous thoughts and threw my arms around my friend.

"OMIGOD!" I squealed, "I'm so happy for you. When did he do it? How did he do it? Did he get on one knee? He'd better have gotten on both knees and begged you."

Karyn exhaled, acting as if the weight of the world had been pulled off of her shoulders.

"Seriously, are you okay with this? I didn't want to tell you because of Crai…Uh, because of everything you've been going through. I didn't want to upset you."

I looked into her hopeful eyes and said, "Of course I'm happy for you. This is so exciting!"

Slowly a smile started on her face and moved up to her eyes. She lit up like I'd never seen before and she threw her arms around me.

"Thank you, thank you, thank you! It was killing me to not tell you, but it was such crap timing so I've kept it all inside."

"Wait, how long have you been engaged?"

"Um, well..ah…"

"Karyn, how long have you been engaged?"

"Since the day you told us about you and Craig," she said quietly, once again looking in her lap as she twisted the life out of her napkin.

"Oh." Ouch.

The table was so quiet, everyone trying to gauge my reaction. Hell, I was trying to gauge my reaction. As much as it hurt, and damn, it hurt; it wasn't about me. I was happy for her, as much as I hurt that it wasn't me. I made up my mind, I let it go.

"Sweetie, I'm pissed that you thought I wouldn't be able to handle it, and that I wouldn't be thrilled for you. I'm so freaking happy for you. It's about damn time, too. But, there's one thing you'd better know right now…" I had my most stern face possible on.

She flinched a little, like she was a little nervous about what I might say. Everyone else at the table leaned forward, concerned I was going to blow a gasket and require a visit from the nice men who would bring me a white jacket with extra-long sleeves.

"I hope you know that I expect to be in the wedding in some ugly-ass dress you pick for your bridesmaids, and not stuck sitting in a hard church pew."

It seemed as if the whole restaurant let out a collective breath of relief. I grinned at my friends, as we all raised our coffee mugs in a cheer to Karyn and Chris' future marriage.

"Ugly-ass dress? You know I have better taste than you, so you know that my brides are going to be fabulous and fierce, working the aisle like rock stars...but not nearly as fabulously as I will. And I expect all three of you bitches to be in my wedding. No maid of honor for me, because there is no way I could pick one of you to do that. You three are more like sisters to me than my own sisters are. You will all be up there with me, and no one else."

We whooped up a few cheers and excitedly started talking wedding plans. I felt the tension in my stomach start to uncoil, and the slight resentment ease away. I could do this. I would do this, and Karyn was never going to know that I wished it was me. Oh, God, how much I wished it was me.

"So what were you all talking about before I walked up and you went all psycho quiet on me?"

"We were thinking about starting dress hunting after coffee." Alex tilted her head and looked at me, "you in?"

"Hellz yeah." I said, "Wait, do you have a wedding date yet?"

"October 10th" she said sheepishly.

"It's just now May. That's a really short amount of time to plan a wedding. Um, not to be rude or anything, but, are you pregnant, Kar?"

"Jeez, NO! I can't believe you automatically went there. No, I am not pregnant. But I'm also not getting any younger, and we would like to have more than one kid. So we figured we'd have a quick engagement, get married and ditch the birth control. And then we are going to have the best time ever trying to make us some gorgeous babies."

We all cackled at that. October 10th, huh? Ten ten. Sounds like a good enough date to get married. Who knows, maybe it would be a lucky wedding date and in no time at all we will be celebrating their fortieth anniversary together as a bunch of old broads. The thought made me smile.

"Dresses, then. Any idea what type of style you are interested in?"

The rest of the coffee meeting was spent discussing mermaids, princesses and a-lines, whether she liked ruching across the front or not, straps or sleeveless.

We linked arms as we left the coffee shop, practically skipping as we went to Karyn's car, piling in like a bunch of young girls going to our first boy band concert. We went to Plymouth to go dress shopping, always enjoying any excuse to be on the historic waterfront.

Karyn led the way into the bridal shop, walking in like a celebrity with her entourage. We were met at the door by a beautifully dressed, wonderfully flamboyant hunk of a man. I fell instantly in love. Brad welcomed us, fawning over 'his' bride. We were whisked into a consultation room, where we were presented with mimosas. I may have to marry him, even if he wasn't exactly into my 'type'. Champagne, even when unfortunately laced with orange juice, was a great way to this woman's heart.

Brad listened to everything Karyn said about her day, what she wanted for styles and started bringing out dress after frothy dress. He also kept the mimosas topped off. At the eleventh dress, we were all starting to get a little tipsy, laughing and talking too loud. We may have one point been singing poorly off key. I think it's possible that I may have proposed to Brad, but no one will confirm or deny.

Finally, Karyn stumbled out of the dressing room wearing a dress that stole everyone's breath and sobered us up quickly. Okay, mostly sobered us. Close fitting to her hips and billowing fabric from her thighs down, she stepped up onto the round little stage, spinning slowly and smiling at all of us. Her breath caught when she saw herself in the mirror. Her arms dropped to her side, and all of our eyes filled up with tears, even in tough-as-nails Alex's.

"Oh my God, Kar." Leah squealed, as she jumped up to run and hug her. We all joined her, a group hug that became a mess of crying, squealing and jumping women. And Brad. Somehow we roped Brad into the hug. Alex may have grabbed his butt. So did Leah, and me, and Karyn. I blame the mimosas, which he kept bringing us, which really means it is his own fault that his butt got grabbed by four semi drunk, slightly hysterical women.

"This is it, ladies, this is the dress that I will become Mrs. Christopher Smyth in."

The schedule for her fittings and alterations were made, and we promised to be back soon to start looking at the bridesmaids' dresses. I think poor Brad cringed a little at the thought of all of us in the room together again. I felt a little bad for him. Okay, not really. This was too much damn fun.

We left, and when I looked at my phone I was shocked to see that it was past lunchtime. We decided to go down to the waterfront and indulge in some overpriced food. I normally stay away from such places, but for my girl, I would put my personal disdain for such things aside. I ordered the salmon and when it came out I was shocked at how much I loved the preparation. This was a stunning presentation of a maple glazed salmon on an almond risotto. The flavors melted in my mouth, blending beautifully a symphony. My friends were watching me as my eyes rolled to the back of my head.

"Oh my Gawd, who needs men when there is food like this out there? I think I just had my first non-battery operated orgasm in three weeks!"

Laughter sounded from all around the table, once they got over the fact that yes, I just said that. Out loud.

I heard a throat clear behind our table. Our teenaged busser was standing there, pale as a sheet, with a pitcher of water. "Refills?" he managed to squeak out. Obviously he heard me. Oops.

"Um, yeah, we'll all take some water."

He scrambled to fill all of our glasses and high-tailed it out of there in record time.

We all looked at each other. I could feel my cheeks burning. A moment of silence and more laughter. I raised my glass of 100 proof water and toasted our girl, Karyn.

By the time I got home, my abs hurt from laughing so much. I think I found a much more preferable way to get my four pack abs. I collapsed on the couch, still grinning as I thought about the fun day we had. I had a blast with the girls all day long, and even at the over-priced restaurant. I groaned again as I thought about that mouth-watering meal I enjoyed. Maybe I'd been wrong. Yeah, I could make great food, but there was something different about having amazing food prepared for you, and all you had to do was sit back enjoy the food, enjoy the company and not have to clean up a messy kitchen afterwards. Huh. I hate admitting that I may have been wrong…good thing I don't have anyone here to admit it to.

I heard a little 'mrowl' from upstairs, and went upstairs with my Kindle to spend the rest of the night with my little family. Penny walked over and niffed my fingers, no doubt she smelled the salmon on me. My hand got a quick sandpaper bath, and she gave me a look that said, "What, no leftovers for me?" I have to start remembering to start bringing home a bite or two for her. This was starting to be my favorite way to end the day. A book, a glass of wine and telling my cats about my day. The kittens were too young to do anything but be ridiculously cute, but I liked to think that Penny enjoyed doing something other than nursing and washing her babies, even if that thing was chatting with me. I made a mental note to schedule an appointment with the vet so that everyone could get checked out and on a vaccination schedule.

I crawled into bed, finally exhausted after the events of the day. The sadness that I initially felt because it was Karyn getting married and not me was gone, completely gone. I smiled, because I didn't want to be 'that person'. I was happy for her, truly happy, and I was thinking that this was going to be a fun wedding to plan. I chuckled a little as I started to drift off. I heard a soft mew and said, "all's good, Penny, go to sleep, baby girl." I fell asleep to the sound of a rumbly purr coming from my closet.

Chapter 6

I found myself amazed at how quickly time went by sometimes. For example, it seemed as if I had just stepped foot into the classroom, walked out, and then walked back in again. That was how fast this week went. But there I was, again, pushing the door open, wondering two things: what was the class going to bring, and what on earth were those friends of mine going to come up with this time.

Mark walked in, five minutes late as expected, and tossed his man bag on the desk. His desirability dropped a few notches in my mind. There was nothing sexy about a man who carried a bigger purse than I did. Okay, there were still some sexy parts about him. I need to either stop thinking about what parts of him were sexy, or I needed to get laid. Or both. Probably both. Damn you, Craig. I sent a mental curse out into the universe, hoping it would somehow get to him.

"An important thing for us to discuss today," started Mark. "If you have hopes of fame and fortune as the world's most prominent blogmeister, you need to interact with your followers. Interact, as in, reply to. You all are here, because you felt a need to learn how to set up and manage your own blogs. You have paid for the opportunity to spend an hour and a half with me every Monday evening for six weeks. That being said, I'd appreciate it if you didn't just go through the motions. What do I mean? Well, every one of you did accomplish the bare minimum for the week's assignment. You wrote a blog. Yippee, gold star for you. However, not a single one of you interacted with any comments to your posts, nor did you reply to emails sent to you. How would I know this?" Mark stalked back and forth in front of us, his hands in his back pockets. "I know this because I commented on all of your posts. I sent all of you emails. I didn't get a single response. I even did a quick double check before coming in today, still no responses. Guys, don't waste my time please. I'm not making a million dollars being here, and I'd enjoy camping out on my couch watching some crap reality show with a beer in my hand more than talking to myself every Monday night."

After that dressing down, I wasn't about to make eye contact with him. I looked around the room, everyone was fidgeting in their seats, uncomfortable with the fact that they were treating this as a way to spend time, as opposed to a way to grow. Yeah, we were all guilty.

My phone chimed with an incoming message. Hmmm, Leah. I'm guessing she's the person in charge of ruining my life this week. WOW, melodramatic much? I decide to wait until after class to check my message.

The class went by quickly, with all of us dutiful students interacting and contributing like we hadn't before. Mark's speech hit the mark.

As I was packing up my stuff, I felt a presence near me. A tall, very masculine presence. One that smelled way too damn delicious for my own good. Drool.

I looked up and immediately went into apologetic mode, "Hey, Mark, I'm really sorry I didn't get back to you about the cat stuff. Time just got away from me, I don't want you to think I'm not interested."

He laughed. "Seriously, Ashley, it's not like you're taking this for credit, so you don't need to be so nervous. I just had to shake everyone up a bit, they were getting way too complacent. Have you even read any of the other blogs? Bare minimum. At least yours was worth reading. Speaking of which, how are the kitties doing?"

"They are doing so great! You should see them. Oh wait, here's my phone…" I proceeded to show him about thirty pictures of the kittens and Penny. To his credit, he actually seemed interested. Well, interested for about fifteen of them.

He held up a bag. I looked at him quizzically.

"Cat toys, remember?"

Oh wow, he was serious about that?

"Thanks so much. Your cat, Charcoal was it? Are you sure she or he won't miss the toys?"

"She, and no, she won't miss them. She has more toys than she can play with in nine lifetimes. Spoiled little brat." He had a smile stretched across his face just thinking about his cat. Man, if only I was in the market for a new man. Gorgeous, sense of humor, smells good and likes cats.

"I really appreciate it, and I'll take a picture or twenty of the kitties playing."

He cringed. I saw it and started laughing at him.

"Oh my gosh, you are too easy. I know I bored the crap out of you with the cat pictures, how 'bout this time I just tell you how the critters liked them?"

Mark's sky blue eyes smiled before his lips did. Then my undoing – the smile crinkles around his eyes – came out. "That sounds perfect." Was it just me or did his voice drop a few notes. I felt something swirling around my lady bits. Uh-oh, not going to happen.

"Uh, awesome, thanks again. I'm sure the puss…uh, I mean, the cats will love it. Um, yeah, Thanks."

Well, that was not the most graceful exit any person has ever made. I swear, if I did real face slaps as often as I did mental face slaps my forehead would either have a permanent bruise or would have an indent. I pictured that for a moment, which sent me into a fit of giggles. So much for appearing 'normal', whatever that was.

I slipped out the door and found a quiet, Wi-Fi accessible spot so that I could find out what form of torture was planned for me this week.

I opened up the email, and saw that it was from Leah this week. I had my fingers crossed in hopes that it was sober Leah not 'I've had a couple drinks' Leah. My eye scanned the words and my heart plummeted.

"Hey, Ash… I don't want to upset you, but your look has been tired for a while, close to a decade. You haven't had highlights, a facial, a new wardrobe or new shoes for over five years. GASP! If nothing else, the lack of new shoes is a crime against humanity. So, my challenge to you is a makeover, but not just any make over… hair-cut, hair color, makeup, five outfits for work, two outfits for a night out and two outfits that are slutty of nature. Oh, and the best part, these are all my choice, not yours. That's this week's adventure. I hope you remember to buckle your seatbelt, this is going to be one hell of a ride."

I added one more forehead slap to my running mental total. Okay, so this version of Leah was a dangerous combo…not quite sober, not quite drunk. She was stuck in that in between stage where the sky was the limit and she was feeling quite limber and bulletproof.

I took a few… maybe several…okay at least twenty deep cleansing breaths. A makeover, I could handle that. A makeover where my friends who were at questionable levels of sobriety got to choose the outcome? More terrifying than watching a horror movie in an antique home with no lights on a windy night. Oh, and with a serial killer on the loose. Yeah, it was that level of hell that made my worst nightmares seem like a day a kid's amusement park.

I picked up my phone and called Leah.

"Okay, you're on." I shout, once she picks up the phone.

"Awesome! This Saturday is our day."

"Perfect, I'll schedule the hair appointment with Ber-"

"Oh hell no, you had BETTER not be thinking that I'm going to let you have your makeover with Bernice."

"Lee, she's been doing my hair forever, I trust her." I was starting to go into panic mode. I mean, full on, hyperventilating, plane's going down, grab the white baggie and start breathing into it hyperventilating mode.

I probably should have explained why a makeover courtesy of my friends scared the shit out of me.

Alex has tried every color in the rainbow for hair colors. Pink highlights, blue highlights, green highlights… you get the picture. Leah has done every funky version of a bob you could possibly imagine, including the asymmetrical one. Right now she had grown her hair out a bit, but had shaved kind of a circle around her head. If she had her hair down, it looked normal. When she had it pulled up into a ponytail, she looked like a bad ass. Karyn, while not adventurous with her hair, could put together outfits that I had to admit look stunning on her, but the mixture of color and patterns would make me look like a clown that got lost on her way to the circus. With the exception of my horrible experiments with bangs and highlights, I tended to wear my hair one of three ways: natural curl/frizz, ponytail or bun. I have been known to go all crazy and flat iron my hair into submission; but that is not a common occurrence a) because I didn't have the time and b) because I didn't want to be bald by the time I was in a nursing home.

"Yes, she's been doing your hair since you were five, which is why you have the same hairstyle that you've had since you were five. No. You will not be going to Bernice. You will be going to Bernard at Hott. You're trading up…old Bernie for new Bernie. But don't call him Bernie, he gets really upset when people call him Bernie. It's not pretty. Sweetie, you need to get your shit shook up. No. More. Bernice."

I started shaking a little at the thought of walking away from my beloved hair stylist. I mean, we've been together forever. I wasn't kidding since I said that I'd been going to her since I was five. Which meant that for every life milestone, Bernice has been there. She just knew me better than anyone else. I felt like I was cheating. I already mentioned that I am not the cheating type, and I felt like I was cheating on sweet old Bernice. Sure, her eyesight isn't what it once was, but it's really hard to screw up long, somewhat frizzy, curlyish hair. It will just stay frizzy and curlyish, and no one would ever know if the cut was wrong.

So, because there's nothing you can do with my hair, I just had always grown it out. Long. Layers sometimes, less layers other times. Bangs sometimes, until that one bitch of a 'stylist' gave me 1980 Sarajevo bangs. You know, not the cute wispy ones, the bangs that start in the middle of your head and fall like the iron curtain across your forehead. I felt fearsome with those bangs, and that is NOT what I was going for. See, that's why stick with Bernice. She would never have given me bangs that screamed 'back in the USSR'.

Then I thought about the time I decided to be trendy and get highlights. Everyone got highlights, so I wanted highlights. I walked out of the salon feeling pretty good that day with my blonde highlights shimmering through my red hair. Then the roots started growing out and it just looked weird. So I went to get it all touched up, and slowly, over time, with touch up after touch up, I had become blonde. No more red hair…all blonde hair. I already had a pale enough complexion, blonde hair was not helpful.

Oh, and that one fancy schmantzy salon I tried once, I found out that the stylist had written a note about me in the system that said 'Mega hair, schedule double time for this one'. Mega hair. Made me sound like some form of a stylist super villain.

Nope, I liked going to Bernice, and I'd had no intention to change my stylist again until the three musketeers ganged up on me.

I resigned myself to the fact that I would be at the mercy of Bernard-not-Bernie, and blocked out my calendar for the weekend. I made a mental note to pick up some cabernet sauvignon on the way home. I had a feeling that I was going to need it.

***

My week went by as it always does. I would love to make myself sound like a ridiculously interesting person, but the truth is, I manage a payroll department. Yeah, I know, right…no wonder I had fantasies of being someone who saves the day wearing a cape. I, instead, saved peoples' paychecks from their own stupidity (i.e., forgetting to clock in or out, forgetting to change their tax forms, forgetting to update their address). I've always thought it was hysterical when people ask what I did that day, because in my head I wonder, 'do you really want me to tell you what I did today, or do you want me to make it sound more interesting than having double checked new hire paperwork and tax forms for over one hundred new hires that start next week at our new location?'

The thing is, I liked my job. It may not be exciting, but it kept me busy and the days went by so fast. I could never stand being bored, and I've had jobs where I've sat there twiddling my thumb for hours, trying to make work happen. That was so not my style. I've always preferred having too much to do and not enough time to do it in.

Because my work week sped by, before I knew it I was waking up on Saturday. I woke to the sound of a meowing cat and stretched, felt pretty great about it being my day off, having a day to read and relax all day. Then it hit me; there wasn't going to be any reading and relaxing that day. I groaned and moved to get out of bed. I checked quickly to see how the cats were doing.

"MROWL!"

"Jeez, Penny, I'm on it. Can't a girl get one day to sleep in?"

I heard a noise come from the closet that seemed as if she disagreed. I scurried downstairs to get her a can of cat food, because those babies of hers were draining her. I knew they were getting great nutrition from her because they were getting chubby while she was slimming out. As soon as she saw the plated food, her rusty purr came in nice and loud.

"Oh, so I guess we're friends now, huh?"

I looked in on the kittens, their eyes were open and so super cute. The all had blue eyes which was adorable. I read, however, that all kittens have blue eyes and that the color would change as they got older. Pity. I've always thought blue eyed animals were something extra special.

I padded back downstairs for my first caffeine infusion of the day, breathing in the thick aroma of my extra dark, almost espresso brew. I swear, there was no smell on earth as heavenly as the coffee container when you first open it. I looked at the clock. 7:30am. Groan. I told the girls I'd meet them at Hott for 9:00am. I knew it was an hour and a half away, but I was annoyed because that amount of time might as well have been five seconds once I got my Kindle fired up.

I sat down on the couch, set an alarm on my phone, and started reading; the tale of lairds and English ladies taking my mind away from the nervousness I felt in the pit of my stomach. When the alarm went off what seemed like a second later, I blinked my way out of the safe world I was in and back to reality. Immediately, my stomach started churning.

Knowing the girls, I figured today I would not be getting away with yoga pants and a T-shirt. Especially not going someplace called 'Hott' to get my hair did by a Bernard. So I picked out my favorite pair of well-worn boot cut jeans, a pair of boots, a button down shirt and a fleece vest. I just let my hair do its natural thing so that Bernard would get to see what he was getting himself into. I couldn't help but wonder if he may have lost a bet. I pictured myself going in with a baseball cap on, and when he was ready for me pulling the cap of as my hair poofed out. In my mind he would shriek, put his hand over his heart and pass out in a dead faint. I started giggling at the mental image, my spirits immediately lifting.

I got to the salon with about five minutes to spare, with the unholy trinity waiting outside impatiently for me. Leah was tapping her foot and Alex started tapping her watch. Jeez, were they really so lonely that they had nothing better to do than torture me all day?

I walked past them and into the salon, the girls trailing me as we walked in. I'm pretty sure I looked like a celebrity with my little entourage. At least, that's how it looked my head.

"Ashley for Bernard, I have a 9:00." I said, in my snootiest, most unaffected voice possible.

"He'll be with you shortly." The girl at the desk gave me a cool appraisal, and then smirked. Crap that meant I did not pass her inspection. Which meant Bernard probably would not be impressed. Oh well, I didn't give a rat's patootie what he thought of me. That's what I kept telling myself, anyway.

"Leah, oh, my darling. I'm so glad you have come to me today."

I heard a lilting voice growing louder as it came closer. When I looked, I was met with a vision of a beautiful man. Not handsome, not sexy, just plain beautiful. Not a hair out of place, a little scruff but not too much, a body that you could bounce quarters off of all day long and never get tired doing it.

"Bernard!" She squealed, jumping into his arms. "We are just so excited to be here today for the first part of the grand transformation of my friend, Ashley."

"I am excited, too, let's see this vision that I will be making great today."

He looked first at Alex with a big smile on his face, she shook her head no. He had a confused look as he turned to Karyn, who grinned and pointed to me. The smile faded as he landed on me and my hair.

"Oh...my..."

I was getting a bit offended, I mean, I know I didn't exactly do my hair and makeup to come have my hair and makeup done, but it's not like I was looking monstrous or anything. I turned up the attitude a bit, hand on my hip and my head cocked, I gave him the once over, slowly, landing at his eyes and spitting out, "well, I guess you'll do."

He looked surprised at first, and then laughed. "Girl, I think I might just love you! So what exactly are we doing today?" He linked his arm with mine and led me to his station, as the girls brought up the rear.

He looked at me expectantly as my friends chimed in with their ideas of what would look good on me. I heard layers, short, buzzed, spiked, color, tint, highlights. All these words were just being thrown around and I just stared ahead. I turned and looked at Bernard and realized he was just watching me, like, studying me while all this was going on. I got the impression that he wanted to know what I wanted, which is the first time in this adventure that my wants had even been thought of. My eyes started to well up a little, which pissed me off because I don't like crying in front of anyone. He caught it though, and I saw him nodding slowly.

"Okay, out you go." I jumped a bit at the sound of his voice, forceful but friendly. I started to get up from my chair, wondering what I had done wrong. I immediately felt a hand on my shoulder. "Not you, them. Leah, you and the gaggle of girls can go somewhere else while I work with Ashley. Give me two hours and come back here. On your way back, I would like a frozen mocha with skim and whipped cream from the coffee shop. Shoo, go..."

I laughed at the looks on my friends' faces, their jaws on the floor with shock that they had been dismissed and would not get to witness my humiliation. They sulked as they walked out of the salon and to the coffee shop, muttering under their breaths and casting searing looks Bernard's way.

Bernard pulled a chair over to me, and turned the salon seat so that I was facing him. "Okay, talk. What the hell is going on?"

I found myself telling him everything, from Craig, to Mark, to kittens and then to this moment. He was wiping tears out of his eyes. "I don't know what part I love best, the fact that you got newborn kitten gak on your favorite shoes, or that your favorite shoes were sensible navy heels. Yes, you need me, but I'm not going to do anything crazy to you, because I'd like you to come back. You have frizzy hair, yes, but that's because you are probably not using the right product, or any product at all."

That last bit was added in as he saw me cringe a little at the word 'product'. Truth was I had tons of product, but I didn't use it. I had purchased various smoothing, softening treatments, but didn't have much luck. So they sat…and sat.

"We're not going short, but we are going to take some dead weight off and add some subtle layers so that it will have fullness throughout, not just at the bottom. I'll be taking off probably about two inches. Stop that! It's not going to be that painful."

I may have whimpered a little. It's possible. Okay, it's probable.

"Also, I love the color, you've got an awesome natural auburn hair. I'd like to kick it up a little with a subtle red toner. This is not anything harsh, we will not be stripping your hair of anything, just adding a little extra something on top. It will look as if you have all sorts of movement and tones in your hair without having to go the highlight route. This way, when your roots grow out, it won't make you look trashy, I promise."

"No bangs?"

"Oh, hell no to the bangs. Your hair is so thick, they will just poof out and look ridiculous on you. My goal is for you to walk out of here with hair you love, not cursing me and going back to the 80 year old who has been doing your hair since you were five."

"She's not eighty."

"Uh-huh."

"More like seven-five." I said weakly, trying to defend that sweet lady.

"Mmmmhmmmm. With that, he took himself to the back as he mixed up the magical elixir that promised to turn my hair into something that was worthy of a slow motion walk towards a fan. I practiced shaking my head out, trying to toss my hair so it landed perfectly fanned over one shoulder and across my back. No such luck.

He came out and told me it was time for a shampoo while the toner set. I settled down into the shampoo chair and gave myself over to the relaxing sensations of a massaging shampoo chair, and the scalp massage I was getting as part of the Hott experience. I was so relaxed that I think I may have fallen asleep a little, because what I remember next was feeling moisture at the corner of my mouth. I tried to nonchalantly wipe my face, but when I looked out the corner of my eye, I saw Bernard's lip twitching while he was trying hard not to laugh. Busted. I just hoped I hadn't been snoring.

The time flew by, during which Bernard and I gossiped about everything in the world, my friends, boys and the blog. I watched, my heart sinking as pieces of my hair went flying all over the place. Two inches, he promised. This looked like a lot more than two inches. I took a glance at the floor and nearly threw up. He turned the chair so it was not facing the mirror and bent down to whisper in my ear, "Trust me."

I had no choice. Soon he was slathering a cold mixture on my head. The toner, he explained. It didn't smell rancid like most hair dyes I've experienced. So I just closed my eyes and tried to relax. Tried to trust him.

Before long it was over. He was getting ready to turn me around to look at the results of his work when I heard, "HOLY SHIT!" from the doorway. I looked up like a deer caught in the headlights and saw my three friends staring at me. Leah had Bernard's frozen mocha in her hand, but the three of them stood like statues as they ogled me.

What the hell, I wanted to see, because at this point in time, I wasn't sure if their reaction meant that he hit it out of the park or that I would be hitting him out of the park.

As I saw my reflection in the mirror, my eyes bugged out and I clasped my hand over my mouth. I loved it, truly loved it. He'd taken what was dull and kinda lifeless and added a little oompf to it.

But the best part was that he hadn't made it look so drastically different that it didn't look like my hair. It was me…but better. I did the swoosh test, slightly tossing my hair from one side to the other, it swayed as if it were strands of pure silk.

"Good?" he asked, looking a little nervous for the first time.

"Great." I replied, as I jumped up to give him a hug, and in the process I splashed hair clippings all over his outfit. Oops.

"Awesome, make-up is next." He pulled me over to a little vanity with all sorts of compacts, tube, brushes and combs. It was like a cosmetologist's den of torture. Bernard kept up a running dialog as he dabbed, rubbed, brushed, fluffed and colored me 'beautiful'. I would love to say I paid strict attention to every dab and swipe, but truth be told I was way in over my head. My idea of makeup was mascara and lip gloss.

"Annnnd, Voila!" A ginormous mirror was presented with a flourish, and I found myself sitting with my eyes closed. I know he did a great job with my hair, and it looked slammin'. But I found that I was scared to have a clownish appearance like when I got a makeup consult at the department store.

"You don't look like a clown, I promise." I looked up at Bernard, one eyebrow up. How the hell did he know I was thinking that? He just laughed at me.

"Quit being a wus and just look at yourself." He commanded. I looked in the mirror and just started grinning. No, I didn't look like a clown, thank God. Once again, I looked like a better version of myself. I would still recognize myself out of a lineup, but would want to take this version out for dinner and dancing. And other stuff…lots of other stuff.

I hated admitting I was wrong about things. Really hated it. But I had to admit, Leah and the girls were totally on point that I needed a bit of therapy for my hair and a makeup lesson. I felt guilty, however, as I stood up front ready to make an appointment for next time. I cringed as I thought about poor Bernice, and how devastated and lonely she would be without my company every eight weeks. Okay, maybe that's a little bit of overkill, but still, she and I had been together for so long.

I paid for my makeover, cringing a bit at the price tag of a color consultation, haircut, toner, makeup lesson and application and all of the makeup I would need to recreate this. Mentally, I thanked

Bernard for the chart he gave me that showed what I was to put where, because I know I never would have figured it out on my own. I remember being baffled looking at the eye shadow compact with three colors. Why three? Just a single color was more than my norm. I snuck a glance in the mirror at the front desk and thought, yeah, that's why there's three colors, so my eyes look like that.

I set the appointment, and figured I'd probably go and schedule an appointment to get my hair trimmed with Bernice, and just come here for the toner refresh, that way I didn't feel so bad about 'cheating' on my long time stylist.

"Bye, Bernard." the four of us sing-songed in unison, waving as we walked out the door.

"Bye, ladies. Oh, and Ashley, you'd better not be planning to go back to your now-former stylist, not even for a trim. I'd hate to have to re-fix everything every eight weeks when we see each other.'

"Uh, okay, yeah, of course" I stuttered as I stumbled out the front door. Seriously, how did he do that?

Chapter 7

After a brief debate, it was decided that shoes would be next, because it would take the least amount of time. I wasn't too scared about shoes, and besides, I needed to replace those heels that the kittens were born on, and that my friends sent up as a burnt offering to the pleather gods.

We went to the local shopping center where there was a huge shoe super-store. I walked in feeling overwhelmed, while the girls looked as if they had died and gone to heaven. Karyn actually put her hand over her heart. I wasn't sure but it appeared as if her eyes were glistening with unshed tears. I didn't get it, I never understood why women went so ga-ga over shoes. Shoes were a necessity, something that helped protect your feet and were hopefully comfortable in the process. Watching my girls as they gazed about the store in rapture had me shaking my head as I plowed forward.

"C'mon guys, we don't have enough time to stand here staring at the shoes. How do you guys want to do this?"

Leah shook her head as if coming out of a trance. "Right, I think we should all branch out and each find two pair of shoes for her. One pair of flats and one pair of heels."

The ladies took off as if someone had fired a shot at the starting line. I meandered through the aisles, trying to see if I could find a replacement pair of shoes for my trusty navy heels. I'm sure I could figure out how to purchase them without the girls noticing. Or maybe come back another day and grab them. Surely I wasn't the only person in the world who based their shoe purchase on comfort and practicality as opposed to looks and sassiness? I had a hard time finding navy blue anything, let alone a low to mid-sized heel that wasn't a stiletto or kitten. Sigh.

"Ashleeeeeeeeeey" I heard from the other side of the store. Oh Lord, they are embarrassing even when they're sober.

I scurried over to where the ladies had gathered, each hugging their shoe selections. Each of them seemed way too eager to have me try on the shoes. I walked over as if my feet were encased in cement and I was on my way to the execution chair. I think I may be the only female in the world who would consider shoe shopping a torturous event.

I started trying on pair after pair, not in love with any of them, as they really said more about my friend's personality rather than mine. The flats were my favorites, so they all ended up in my 'keep' pile. Karyn was kind enough to pick out a pair of heels that weren't super high, they were black leather with a subtle pattern. The heel wasn't obscenely high, and while stilted, I could walk in them. I begrudgingly pushed them into the okay pile.

Leah's pair of heels I knew right off I wouldn't be taking. I had nothing that would go with baby pink heels with black polka dots on it. I did think they were kind of cute, I mean, the heel was a black patent leather and it had ankle strap, but again, not something I had anything to wear with. I tried them on and I was a bit wobbly, but I managed. I discreetly pushed them away from the other shoes, though, because I didn't want to hurt Leah's feelings.

Alex stood in front of me with a shit-eating grin on her face. Oh, no. Once she had everyone's attention she whipped the top off of the shoe box, and I found myself staring at some really beautiful shoes. They had a black and white floral pattern on them, and were made of a cloth type material, not of leather. I was super excited to try those on, they were gorgeous and would go with almost everything. Then Alex pulled one out of the box and turned it sideways and I almost screamed. Those beautiful shoes had about a four and a half inch heel on them. I was pretty sure she was trying to kill me.

"Are you trying to kill me?"

"Oh, come on, they aren't that bad! I know they look super tall, but they have a little half inch platform in the front, so they aren't as tall as they seem."

Okay, so they are now four inch heels as opposed to four and a half inch heels. They might as well be four feet tall for all the good that half inch platform would do me.

"Get 'em on and walk the freaking runway, beyotch!"

At this point in time we were getting a bit of attention. Apparently four women battling over shoes was a sight to behold, especially when one of us was so hell bent on not trying on the shoes in question.

"Fine, fine, I'm getting them on."

I put the shoes of death on my feet and braced myself on my friend's shoulder as I steadied. I may have leaned extra weight on her than was necessary, judging by the 'oof' sound she made. Oh, my bad.

My steps forward were very cautious. You've seen little four year old girls trying on their mommy's high heels? You know how they walk and it's more a 'clomp, clomp, clomp' than a 'heel, toe, heel, toe'? Yeah, it was like that for me. With a crowd gathered and watching me make my way across the store. Clomp. Clomp. Clomp. A Clydesdale horse would have had more grace than me balancing on those ice picks mistakenly marketed a shoes.

I started to wobble a little less and heard some words of encouragement from the gathering of fellow shoppers.

"Looking good."

"Now you're getting the hang of it."

"Those shoes are hot on you."

I made my pivot turn very slowly and started to walk back. I realized these shoes didn't hurt as much as I'd thought they would, and I think between that and the catcalls from my adoring new fans I may have put a little extra sway in my hips as I walked back. I fancied myself a supermodel on the cat walk. I leaned back a little with my shoulders, hips forward and swinging back and forth. In my head I pictured the flashing of lightbulbs from the paparazzi as I walked by. This elevated confidence was to be my undoing.

Perhaps I hadn't mentioned this, but I had a genetic predisposition to clumsiness. When Craig referred to me as 'Grace' , it wasn't because of my qualifications to be a ballerina. No, if there was an accident to be had, I would find it. I took after my dad that way. So there I was, starting to sashay and shimmy my hips and work that cheap carpet in the shoe store when suddenly it happened. My left ankle wobbled left, and when I tried to correct it my right ankle twisted, and I stumbled forward, somehow falling over the bench that was there for me to try on these evil demon shoes. When I opened my eyes, six people were bending over looking at me, I was on my back with my legs up on the bench, the Satan shoes elevated in all their maniacal glory.

"Oh my God...are you okay?"

I turn my head and see my friends trying to look concerned, but failing miserable for the fact that they were bent over laughing too hard at my predicament.

"Hate. You. So. Much."

I kicked the purveyors of pain off of my feet and started to stand up. Holy mother of God, that hurt. I looked at my feet and saw that my right ankle was starting to get a little swollen. I limped over to Alex, pointing at her with my most evil facial expression possible.

"This is your fault. You forced me to walk in those…those. .."

"My fault? Nope. You chose to walk in them, I don't recall having a single gun to your head." She turned and flounced away from me, grabbing the shoes that had been discarded and bringing them to the front to purchase.

I limped about, grabbing the shoes I would buy, gratefully pushing Leah's choice under a rack. The one good thing about my performance is she had long since forgotten the pink shoes that she chose. As I made my way to the register, all of those people who were my adoring fans just seconds ago couldn't make eye contact. Sigh. Fame is so fleeting.

The car ride to lunch was extremely quiet. Well, quiet except for the intermittent snort of laughter. I was pretty sure that I had master the 'I freaking hate you' look, as not a single one of them said a word to me when we were in the car.

When we got to the restaurant, I got out of the car first, slamming the door as I heard them burst into peals of laughter. I limped with as much indignation as I could muster up as I strode into the restaurant. Making a beeline for the ladies room, I took my sneaker and sock off to inspect the damage. There wasn't too much swelling, just a bit of poofiness. I pressed around the ankle and while sore, it wasn't sharply painful, so I figure I just twisted it pretty bad. I put my sneaker back on and laced tightly to help support my ankle and went to meet the hyenas at the table.

"…going to kill us."

I cleared my throat and three sets of eyes snapped to me with a look of fear in them. Hmm, interesting. What on earth had I interrupted?

"Um, so, to make up for the whole sexy-as-hell shoe incident, I'm going to cover your lunch today." That was Alex.

I grunted, wanting to tell her that this pathetic attempt at patching things up was not going to work, but I'd spent so much on hair, makeup and shoes, that I could use a small break.

"Listen, Ash, we're really sorry you go hurt. And that we laughed. We're really sorry that we laughed. But in our defense, we did ask if you were okay first."

I gaped at them, full on fishy open-mouthed gaping. Seriously? They thought that asking if I was okay made up for the bruising my backside and my pride took?

Three sets of the saddest most pathetic puppy dog eyes pointed my way, and I felt my resolve slowly crumble.

"Okay, okay, I can see where it may have been a teensy bit funny."

All of the girls let out a collective breath, and then the laughter started. By the time we had finished lunch and left I could really see the humor in the whole thing. It was a typical Ashley moment. We went on to shop for clothes and had no more embarrassing mishaps. I dare say I even liked the outfits the girls picked out.

I went home and filled the tub with my favorite lavender laced Epsom salts. Lowering myself into the tub I let out a loud, prolonged groan. That tub felt like heaven, because at this point in the day every part of my body ached. I turned on my spa music station online and started to relax into the tub.

Next thing I knew I heard a loud, obnoxious noise and the water was ice freaking cold. I jumped out of the tub, and quickly remembered my sore ankle. Damn! Someone was ringing my doorbell as if their life depended on it. I reached for my old as sin and equally as ugly terry cloth robe and headed down stairs to investigate.

I peeked through the window and saw my friend sitting there holding out chocolate and a bottle of wine. I wasn't sure what they had done, but if it required red wine and dark chocolate it must be a doozie. I opened the door and gave them my best 'what have you done' look. They filed in past me into the living room.

"Hey, yeah, come on in, make yourselves at home." There may have been some snarkiness. Maybe.

Leah popped open the bottle of wine and started pouring while Karyn brought over my favorite dark chocolate on the planet. Alex sort of was fidgeting with her phone. All of those things combine spelled trouble.

"Seriously, guys, what's going on? You're freaking me out."

"Have you been online at all since you've come home?" Alex asked as she headed for my tablet.

"No, I've just been zoned out in the bathtub."

"Listen, I'm sorry. I didn't do this, I didn't post this, and I knew nothing of it."

She handed over my tablet and there was a video ready to go. I pressed play and saw myself sashaying and shimmying at the shoe store. Oh Lord, I didn't realize I did the royalty wave in front of everyone. My horror grew as I watched my left ankle go wonky, my right ankle twist and I saw myself fall backwards over the bench. Whoever took the video chose that moment to zoom into the shoes, and as such caught a glimpse of my legs that were pale as death on a good day.

I planted my forehead into the palms of my hands. Why on earth did this happen? I looked up at them and realized a glass of red was being thrust in my right hand while I suddenly had some chocolate melting in my left. I swallowed the wine down in one gulp. I am sure I mentioned what a lady I am at this point, right? After eating the dark chocolate, which at this point tasted like chalk, I finally spoke.

"Who did that? Who posted that horrible video?"

"No idea, one of the people enjoying the show you put on, obviously. But here's the crazy thing, it's only been up for about two hours, and you already have over ten thousand views. You're becoming a local internet sensation."

I slowly lowered myself onto the couch. I watched the video again with my friends, the three of them moving slowly from anger on my behalf to amusement to a bad case of the giggles.

"Wait a minute." screeched Karyn after the third or fourth viewing. "Your legs! Oh my gawd, the close up of your legs."

The rest of peered closer at the close up in the final frame of the video, then after studying the frame a little bit, Leah and Alex retracted in horror.

"Ashley, how could you?"

"How could I what? What am I missing here?" I tilt my head left, than right, still only seeing two legs dangling over the bench.

"Geez, when was the last time you shaved your legs, woman?"

Oh my Lord, no! I looked even closer and yes, dear God, yes, you could see my leg stubble on the camera. So now, not only was the world finding out how absolutely graceful I was, they were also figuring I was of questionable hygiene.

"Well, why would I have shaved my legs? It's not like I'm going to be showing them to anyone any time soon. As a matter of fact, it's been over three weeks since anyone has seen my legs. Well, until now."

"Ewwwwwwwwwwww." That was a collective from the group.

"Wait, you haven't shaved your legs since Craig left? I should have forced you to do a waxing today." Leah shook her head, in obvious dismay over my apparent neglect of leg hair.

"You do that and you are dead to me. Do you hear me? Dead to me." In all honesty, they weren't high up on my favorite people list currently. That had been one hell of a stressful day.

We finished the bottle of wine and chocolates together, and I ushered them out the door.

I went upstairs to my new favorite place, on my cushion next to my cat family. It was then I finally succumbed to the humiliation of the past day, and the continued pain over Craig. I would have thought that I'd have heard from him by now. While I was indulging in my pity party for one, crying my heart out, I felt a little pat-pat on my left arm. I looked down, and there was my Penny, looking up at me as if she understood the pain of being left behind and the humiliation that life can bring. Well, then again, maybe she did. She was a single mother after all, she experienced a man getting what he wanted from her and then walking away. I started petting her as she rubbed against me. Her purring and the softness of her fur helped make the tears stop. When she climbed into my lap, still purring, I leaned against the wall, just enjoying this quiet moment with my cat. At least the first challenge had turned out great for me. I wiped at my wet eyes, and then went back to petting her. I looked down when I felt sandpaper rubbing the wet spot on my hands where I had wiped my tears. Penny was cleaning my tears from my hand. My heart warmed a bit, and I felt better than the chocolate and wine had made me feel. We sat like that for what seemed like hours, when she heard one of her kittens mewling, she stood up, gave me a head bump, and went back to work raising her family. Sometimes, I really felt as if that cat understood me.

Chapter 8

I woke up the next morning to the sound of the phone ringing. I looked at the clock, holy crap, it was already 8:00am? I never slept in that late. Okay, so perhaps 8:00am isn't considered late to everyone, but I tend to get up early, even on the weekends.

I saw my mother's name on the phone display and quickly picked up. I never missed a call from my mom.

"Honey, why did I see a video of you making a fool of yourself on the morning news today?"

Huh, what?

"What are you talking about, mom?"

"On the news they were talking about a local video gone viral. And then showed a video of you acting like wobbly pageant queen trying on a pair of shoes that you and I both know you shouldn't even be allowed to look at, let alone stand in."

"Oh, Lord, long story. How 'bout I come over later and we can have some hot cocoa and I'll fill you in on everything."

"Sounds like a plan, and while you're here, you can help me clean out the attic."

"'Kay, Mom. See you in a bit". The attic. You have no idea how many times mom had said I'd help her clean out the attic. Yes, she said I would help her clean out the attic. You see, there's still a bunch of stuff from my childhood up there, that I'm not willing to part with, but at the same time don't want in my house. Clutter and all.

"See you then, Ashley Marie." Only my mom could get away with calling me by my first and middle name. I figure it's her birthright. She gave birth to me, therefore she had the right to call me whatever she wanted.

I stretched and pulled my laptop up onto the bed. I figured it was time to update the blog. As I was typing in the events of the day, I decided I was going to put that video in the post. It was easy enough to find, unfortunately, as everyone I know seems to have posted it on their social networking pages, and tagged me in the process. When the original video pulled up, I was shocked to see over sixty thousand views, and that number kept increasing. It was just ten thousand last night. Thanks to the internet, my identity had been figured out, so all hopes of anonymity were out the window. This was not the way I wanted to become famous.

I had to laugh, though. I mean, I always had said in the past that my level of 'gracefulness' was legendary. This was not what I meant. At least I was finally laughing about it, that didn't take too long. I suppose I wouldn't be murdering the girls, after all. Shame.

I copied the embedding code and popped it into my blog. Once I proof-read the entry, my mouse hovered over the 'publish' option. I clicked and then a small wave of panic flew through me. Mark was going to think that I was the world's biggest klutz and probably wouldn't want anything to do with me after seeing this video. But at this point, I wasn't one hundred percent sure if I wanted him to do anything with me, so I decided it was better to let him see all the lump and bumps that made up my life. I clicked 'publish'.

When I moved back to the Wareham area, I specifically chose a house close to my parents. I was super close to them, and wanted to be near them as they got older in case they needed me. Turns out I was able to find a house that was only about a mile away from them, and only a short five minute car ride. I realized that in some circles it was more 'en vogue' to have great disdain for your parents, but I could never quite muster that up. I'd always been a daddy's girl, and I didn't see that changing. Also, my mom was my very best girlfriend. I know that I had my circle of friends, and they were great for discussing the things one should never discuss with their mom. Like their sex life. No one, and I mean no one should ever discuss their sex life with their mom or dad. It's just, well, wrong.

I walked in the front door, yelling "Helllooooooooo".

Mom came bounding down the stairs and hugged me as if she hadn't seen me in months, let alone a couple weeks. "It feels like I haven't seen you in forever."

I laughed, "Mom, it's only been a couple of weeks, not really a forever. Besides, I only live about a mile away, it's not like I live in Iowa."

We sat down over cocoa, and I filled her in on everything since Craig left. She squealed appropriately at the part of the cats, and demanded that she be allowed to come over and visit her new grandbabies. I reminded her that she has a key and can come over whenever she wants.

The smell of cocoa and the sound of conversation brought my dad downstairs. He came over to give me a hug. "Hello, Ashley-gator." I grinned at the childhood nickname.

"Hi, Daddy. Are you going to have some cocoa with us?" Yes, I still called him Daddy. A girl should never get so old that her father stopped being Daddy.

"Sounds good."

Mom popped up to make him a hot cocoa, and threw quite a few extra marshmallows in, just the way he liked it. So you know, it's not like my parents' home is stuck in the 1940's. Mom is just like that. If someone needs/wants something, she always does it for them. She's all kinds of awesome, but I always worried that she should let people do stuff for her every once in a while.

"So, Ashley was just telling me that she has a cat and kittens in her house."

Dad turned and looked at me, surprise and delight filling his eyes. My dad had always had a soft spot for cats. I pulled out my phone and they both ooohed and ahhhhhed over the photos of the momma cat and her babies.

"You can come over and see them anytime."

We chatted about everything and nothing, avoiding the topic of Craig altogether, because it was still a sore spot for me. I wondered if that would ever change, or if as long as our relationship was in this weird limbo would I still ache at the mention of his name.

Mom stood up, started collecting mugs, and announced that it was time to clean out the attic. Oh man, I was hoping that she'd forgotten about that part. I helped clean up the mugs and spoons and put them away as we trudged upstairs. I was surprised to see my dad joining us, he usually found a reason to disappear when a cleaning project was on the table. He had an amazing ability at remembering projects he had somehow forgotten until that very moment, such as replacing a light bulb, or cleaning a secret, remote corner of the basement Mom and I must not know about; because we've certainly never seen any part of the basement cleaned by Dad's hands.

I was glad it was the end of May, because it hadn't gotten too hot up in the attic, yet. It's not like my parents would bother heating or cooling up in the attic, so we have this small window of opportunity in April and May, or late September to beginning of November to get the attic done. We all started working on our various boxes, and I'm pretty sure we spent more time reminiscing than actually putting together piles of what would be thrown out, what would be donated, and what would be brought to my house.

We spent several hours up there, and I had to admit, it was fun. I was having a great time with my folks and it was a blast seeing all of my old stuff.

I looked over my shoulder and saw a smaller box that was sealed up tight. I reached for it and started to cut open the tape. I saw something white and fluffy underneath and figured it was another one of my old stuffed toys.

"Hey, guys, I found another box." I said, as I started to pull out what was inside. What happened next was sort of in slow motion in my mind.

"NO!" My mom and dad shouted at me in unison. Although, in my head I heard "Nooooooooooooooooo" in a long, drawn out deep voice, like in the movies when something goes slo-mo.

I gave them a confused look and then turned my attention to what I was holding out in my hands. My eyes stung. I would never be able to unsee what I was seeing. I was holding up a barely there, Mrs. Claus teddy, complete with faux fur trim. When I'd pulled it out of the box, a matching man's g-string style undergarment thing fell out along with a pair of red lace teensy panties. I looked at my parents and back to the teddy about five times, my face frozen in a look of horror that I'm pretty sure matched the look on my parents' faces. I threw the teddy and pieces back into the box, being very careful not to touch certain parts of it. I was not about to touch anything that had touched my parent's neatherlands. Full body involuntary shudder. I packaged that box up tighter than Fort Knox and threw it across the room.

There was deadly quiet in the attic. No one could make eye contact or speak.

I finally cleared my throat and looked up at mom and dad. Their faces were both burning red.

"We shall never speak of this moment ever again." I said quietly. They nodded solemnly. We all quickly went back downstairs and I headed straight to the bathroom. I scrubbed my hands as if I was about to perform open heart surgery. I scrubbed my hands so hard they started to hurt, but I had to get the cooties from mom and dad's sex outfit off of my hands. Yes, I said cooties. Deal with it. I then started splashing water in my eyes. I know it didn't do anything, but I was trying to convince myself that it was bleach that I was splashing in my eyes, and that it would remove the memory from the attic. No such luck. Another involuntary full body shudder. Remember when I said that kids should never talk to their parents about their sex lives? Well, that goes both ways. I could have lived a million years without knowing that my parents had engaged in some reindeer games.

I went downstairs, hugged and kissed my folks and headed out to my car. It was then I realized that I didn't have anything from the attic. No box for donation, nothing to go into storage at my house. We had left everything upstairs. Which means, we had accomplished nothing. I started laughing. I bet she wouldn't volunteer me to help clean out the attic for quite a while. SCORE!

***

While I did experience some glee in knowing that I would not get stuck cleaning their attic, there was a weird feeling finding out that my parents were still sexually active at their age. On one hand, I was thrilled that they were obviously still attracted to each other and in love; but on the other hand – what child doesn't believe that they were somehow immaculately conceived? I didn't necessarily think that my conception was immaculate; but had thought (hoped) that maybe they got drunk one night, got frisky and thus I came into existence. But in my version, they didn't particularly enjoy the process. So, even though the coupling was less than awesome, they realized they'd had a tiny miracle and were thrilled with the end result of their drunken debauchery. Thrilled, but never inclined to have sex. Ever. Again.

You know I had to tell someone about this. I mean, had to. But if not all three of my friends, at least one. Now who could possibly get the most enjoyment of my humiliating moment with my parents, I wondered. A slow, almost evil smile curled my lips. Oh my God, she was going to die. I took out my phone and called Alex.

Two rings and she answered. "Girl, you are never going to believe what happened today at my parents' house."

I told her the whole story. She pretty much let me get through it without interrupting (oh, minor miracles) but "oh my God" and "holy shit" were peppered throughout.

When I finished my recounting there was dead silence on the other end of the phone. At first I thought perhaps we had gotten disconnected. Then, all of a sudden, laughter. Huge, unsexy, guffaws of laughter. And then a snort.

"Well, it could have been worse." Alex said, once she had caught her breath.

"How on earth could that have been worse? I touched something my parents wore while getting spanky spanky with each other?"

"It could have been a lot worse. First, you could have walked in on them getting down."

"Oh, Lord, that would have been cause for psychotherapy, right there."

"Second, my little head case, you could have opened that box and found their assortment of bondage and BDSM paraphernalia, as well as their favorite porns."

I couldn't think after that mental image entered my mind. I think the only sound that came out was a squeak.

More laughter came from the other end of the phone. "Holy shit, I rendered Ashley speechless. Miracles never cease."

"Bitch." Yeah, that was my clever comeback. Why couldn't quick wit come into play when I needed it? I figured I would come up with a great retort about ten minutes after we got off the phone with each other. Ugh, I hated when that happened.

"Seriously, though, Ash, that was hysterical. What did your parents do when you pulled out your mom's nasty-wear?"

I laughed, I mean, seriously, at this point in time what else did I have left but than to laugh at the absurdity of the situation.

"So, I read your blog, I can't believe you added the video to it. Aren't you worried about the whole anonymity thing, or what Teacher McHottie is going to think about it?"

"First off, I don't care about all that crap. I figured if people were getting off on me making a fool of myself in high heels....so be it. Second, Teacher McHottie? Have you been binge watching Grey's Anatomy without me again?" The four of us friends have had friendly battles over which of us was going to entice Patrick Dempsey to leave his real-life wife for us. Alex usually won the battles. She really hadn't been the same since his character got killed off of the show. She'd been wearing black an awful lot.

"Your choice, baby girl, Teacher McHottie or Sir Hotsalot. "

"Seriously, what is this, grade school?" Alex had a huge thing about giving people odd nicknames.

"What the hell is wrong with just calling him Mark?"

"If I called him just 'Mark', I wouldn't be getting you so riled up. At least, not nearly as easily. So what's the deal with you two? Are you going to continue in the flirtatious foreplay or actually do the deed?"

"Alex, have I ever told you what a hopeless romantic you are?

"Um, nope."

"GOOD!"

We both laughed a little more. I then sighed and said, "I think he'd be thrilled if I gave the 'all systems go'; but, truth be told, I'm not sure I'm ready to have someone else start my engine yet."

"Car analogies, really, Ashley?" Alex sniffed, raising her chin a notch in an attempt to appear 'above it all'. However, we both knew she was a gear head, who lusted for nothing more than to be the proud owner of a '65 Mustang Convertible. It was a lifelong dream to buy a 'rescue pony' and fix it up. Most people at her age would be saving for a down payment on a house. She was saving for a run-down rust-bucket.

I laughed at her, rolling my eyes at the faux conceit. "Alex, I'm just not ready. I think if I'd heard something from Craig, even a text saying we were truly done, I would jump him quicker than he could roll on the protection. I wish I could be slutty. I wish I could just jump into bed with him and do things to him that would make a prostitute blush, but I can't. I'm a loyal person. It wouldn't be me. I lust for Mark right now, but lust can die in time. I am in love with Craig. That is so much stronger than lust will ever be."

She got really quiet on her end of the phone, probably assessing me. I hated when she did that, it was not an uncommon thing with her. The scary as hell thing, is she usually was successful in her assessment.

"Hmmm, okay. No Mark because of the Craig situation. Got it. Gotta go, now. Bye." Beep. I sat there looking at my phone, surprised by her abrupt goodbye. Alex never was one for big, long, drawn out phone conversations, but that was...different.

I had a weird feeling something a little funky was going on, but this whole day had been funky, so I was probably just being a little mental. Thinking about it, every day since the love of my life did the Macarena on my heart had been nothing short of funky. I smiled, because, truthfully, it had made the past few weeks not only bearable, but kind of awesome. Not that I would ever admit that to my friends.

I shrugged, it was time for kittens. The little cuties were moving around and (yay!) using the litter pan on their own. I couldn't wait for them to eat food, because it hurt to just look at my Penny's nips. Seriously, those kittens have made her boobs so raw. I think that human moms have it so easy. Usually only one baby and they complain about being bit. I think Penny has earned kitty sainthood.

Talking about whether or not I was still with Craig and whether or not I wanted to be with Mark left me feeling a bit out of sorts. You know, kind of sad. I've never been the mope about type of person. I didn't like letting people know when I'm down. I always thought that was the New England side of me, stiff upper lip and all that. But up there, in my bedroom, sitting on a pillow outside my cats' closet; I finally let the sadness have its evil way with me. Sniffling while big, fat tears rolled down my cheeks and splashed on my yoga pants that doubled as PJ bottoms.

I felt a bump on my left arm, and looked down as Penny was head bumping my arm. I gave her a watery smile. She seemed to know I needed some affection. I was just done with being alone. I know I had my friends and all, but I just felt alone. I kept petting Pen's head absently, and when I looked down at her she was giving me a look like she was trying to figure me out.

"Oh God, not you, too? Should I have renamed you Alex, Jr?"

A loud purr erupted from my cat. I swear, she was laughing at me. I would never understand how this cat was so human. Suddenly she turned her head to the closet and let out a short series of very sweet chirpy sounding meows. I was a little worried that something might be wrong with the kittens, until one by one they came out of the closet towards me. Their little legs were not quite sure yet, but they were walking over to their mom, who nudged them closer to me, looked at me and said "Mrowl!" Good God, I wished I could speak cat. I thought perhaps she was telling me to pet one. I reached my hand out and all three wanted attention. I started laughing through my tears at those three little attention whores. I scooped them up and pulled them in for a gentle hug, then set them in my lap. I suddenly didn't feel so alone anymore. My transition to crazy cat lady turned spinster was complete.

"Thanks, Penny, I needed that."

"Mrowl."

Chapter 9

After the crazy weekend I'd had, I wasn't really in the mood to go to class Monday night. Also, I didn't really want to face Mark after posting about my embarrassing shoe shopping excursion and the conversation I'd had with Alex the previous evening, of which he was the major topic. As I walked into the classroom, my phone dinged indicating a message.

I found my seat and checked the time. Five minutes to spare and plenty of time to check my email. I was surprised when it was from Alex. I had just seen her last night, and we weren't usually the needy type of friends who had to be in contact every second of every day. It just looked that way to the outside world. I was pretty sure that there were some in our town who thought we were a crazy group of cult lesbians who were *together* together. We always got some laughs over store owners' initial reactions to us, before they got to know us (and before they got to know that we pay good money to eat and drink at their establishments).

I pulled up the email and started reading.

"Hey Ash, I did a lot of thinking about our conversation last night. Well, a lot of thinking after I got over the mental image of your mom and dad dressed up like the Kinky Clauses. Can I just say 'ew' again? Anyhoo, it's my turn to pick your challenge. So here is this week's challenge. Ask a guy out on a date, and then go on the date with him. Preferably Mark, because there may be something to pursue there. Sweetie, you have got to come to the realization that Craig may not be coming back, and that you may no longer be a part of a 'we'. So please, don't hate me, just ask someone out on a date, specifically Mc Hots A Lot."

I was shaking my head no, and had tears pooled in my eyes. That was the moment that Mark chose to show up. I looked up at him, I'm sure looking devastated and panicked. He tilted his head and looked at me with confusion. The look clearly said 'what is going on.' My shoulders slumped forward a little. I mouthed the word 'after'. A moment passed where I was starting to worry that I imagined his concern, and then a short nod. Yup. After.

I didn't hear a word of class. I looked down at my pad of paper and I had written nothing. I found myself sinking deeper and deeper into my seat. Here's the deal. I was never one to do confrontation. No thank you. It always made my stomach turn queasy. Also, I have always been a bit dumb when it came to reading people. Seriously. My friends would tell me someone was 'into' me, and I just thought they were very nice guys. Not that a ton of people hunted me down, banged down my doors, strapped me onto the bed and had their wicked ways with me. No, nothing like that. But I just wasn't great at reading situations. I swear, someone would have to strip down naked in front of me in order for me to catch on that he was doing more than just saying 'hi'.

Asking someone on a date, however, that put me into a level of discomfort that had my heart racing, and not in a fun, spanky sort of way.

The class went by way too fast. Next thing I knew, I heard the scraping sound of chairs on linoleum. I jerked back to reality and looked up at Mark. Shit, he was looking pretty annoyed at me today. This was not going to be fun. I walked up to the front of the class, like a petulant, pouting three year old. I think I even actually dragged my feet. Yeah, this was going off to a great start.

"Ash, what the hell is wrong with you today? I could tell you weren't paying attention, as a matter of fact you looked as if you wanted to be anywhere but in my class today. After your blog this week, I figured you'd be riding high because of all the hits and the great feedback you received. What gives?"

Feedback? Hits? I made a mental note to get better on follow through.

"Sorry, Mark, it's just that..well…my friend Alex gave me my next 'challenge' for the blog. And..um…it is one that is, uh, going to be challenging, I mean, um… Shit… just read."

I shoved my phone at him, with the email message on it.

I peeked up and watched his face as he read through the message. Surprise, amusement, shock, laughter and then…

"Mc Hots a Lot?" He looked at me, smirking with one eyebrow jacked up.

"Um, oops. Maybe I should have not just had you read that. Sorry, I suck at this. Mark, I'm not ready to date, but I've made all but a blood oath to my friends to do every stupid thing they have come up with for this blog. I have to do it, I can't back down, but I feel like just asking someone on a date is like cheating on my maybe-he-is-maybe-he-isn't boyfriend. But this is like a double dog dare for a guy. So, Mark, will you go out with me? On a date, not like a long term relationship, but maybe just coffee or a drink or something. Oh God, I'm screwing this up so bad." I put my hands over my face, not wanting to see his reaction to my less than suave date request. I spread the fingers of my right hand so that I could see his facial expression and was shocked to see laughter in his eyes. Damn you, sexy as hell eye crinkles.

"So you are going to use me for the blog. Just use me and then discard me? That's your plan?"

"When you put it that way it sounds so…sordid." I knew I was blushing ferociously at this point.

"Wow, I don't know what to say, just, wow. I feel so violated." I whipped my head up to look at him in shock and his face was unreadable.

"Hey, if you don't want to, that's fine. I mean, I'm sure I can find someone else. Crap, that sounded conceited. I mean, I'd rather go with you but I don't want to offend you."

He looked at me a moment, broke into a grin and said, "Pick you up at seven on Sunday. Casual." He started to walk out of the room.

"Wait! I need to give you my address."

"Nope, already got it."

Huh? "How?"

"Enrollment records, my dear."

"STALKER!"

I heard his low, rumbly laughter down the hall as he walked away, and my lady parts clenched a little because it was so sexy. I looked down and scolded myself, "bad lady parts, bad! We are still technically with Craig and we do not cheat. No matter what." I swear, I heard my lady parts crying.

I called Alex as soon as I got to my car.

"You want me to have a one night stand with Mark?"

"I never said anything about a one night stand. I said a date. Date doesn't necessarily mean sex. Unless you're nasty."

UGH. I was feeling pretty damn nasty right about now. "What if he's a murderer? We know nothing about him. I know nothing about him. Now I'm going out on a date with him. What if he's planning on killing me in cold blood and leaving me on the side of the road?"

"Well, I guess it really would just be a one night stand at that point." I could hear the laughter in Alex's voice. She obviously did not take my concern seriously. That bitch.

***

I looked at my bed, literally pulling my hair in desperation as I stared down my clothing choices for tonight's non-date. It shouldn't have been so hard. It wasn't this hard with Craig. This wasn't even a real date, it was more like a dare, a check box that needed to be checked. So why did I care whether I was too dressy, too casual or even too 'lay me down on the table and eat your dessert off of me'. I needed help, because I was a second from calling to cancel. Then I remembered, I didn't have his information, he had mine. Groaning, I flung myself backwards on the bed. I was pathetic.

I picked up my phone and called Leah.

"Hey, Ash, you talking to me again?" I could hear the laughter in her voice. True, I should be NOT talking to her over the whole stiletto stilts situation; but I was desperate. And it's not like I really gave her a decent silent treatment, I'd just been busy.

"I know not of what you speak. I need your help, though. Alex has forced me into a date that I'm not really wanting to go to, and so I have to pick out an outfit that doesn't quite scream hands off but at the same time doesn't say 'take me lover boy'."

I got that all out in a rush of breath, only to have to pull my phone away from my ear to keep from suffering hearing loss with the high pitched squeal coming from the other end of the phone.

"Ohmigawd! You're going on a date with the tasty teacher?"

"Really, Leah, really? Tasty Teacher?"

"No good? Okay, how about the Perfect Professor?"

I rolled my eyes.

"Sexy scholar, tempting tutor, irresistible instructor…I can go all day, Ash." Leah was laughing, you could tell she was so proud of herself.

"Someone's been spending way too much time with Alex. But yes, I'm having dinner with Mark, just Mark, not marvelous Mark or whatever your head was about to do with his name. Can you come over and tell me what to wear?"

"Be over in a sec."

When Leah came over, she walked up to my bedroom and just stood there in shock. Her face actually went pale. I stood back and looked at it to figure out what was so strange, and then I saw it. It looked like a bomb went off in my bedroom for all the clothes that were all over the place. She turned slowly and just looked at me, mouth still open.

"Um, so, I think this may be everything I actually own."

"Yeah, ya think?" Lean quickly walked around my bed, picking things out and putting them back into the closet. While she was working I could hear her muttering things like 'oh hell no', 'seriously' and I think I heard one 'should be burned'. After about fifteen minutes we stood back looking at three outfits. Three. That was good. I could mentally handle three.

"Okay, so where's he taking you?"

"No idea. Not a clue."

Leah tapped her index finger on her scrunched up lips. She nodded, then took one more outfit away and returned it to the closet.

"Ash, be honest with me. Do you want this to be anything? Do you want Mark as a real option? Or are you seriously doing this only for the blog? Because it's not fair to lead him on, so I want to pick the right outfit."

Man, I felt like such a jerk that I was only going on this date to satisfy the blog requirements. He really was too good to be used that way. I hung my head a little.

"If it wasn't still so up in the air with Craig, I'd allow myself to pursue Mark. He's everything I would normally look for in a guy, if only my heart wasn't on hold. He's gorgeous, funny, kind, smart…he seems to be the whole package. But I am in this weird situation, so I can't even think about moving on with someone else yet."

Leah tilted her head and just stared at me for a few seconds. "Yeah, he sounds pretty damned perfect." She actually seemed a little angry at me. She picked up the red dress from the bed and put it back in the closet. What was left was a pair of dark jeans, brown wedge sandals, a light pink scoop neck T-shirt and a thin cardigan. Casual without being too casual.

"Okay, and I'm going to have you cuff the jeans so you can show off the shoes, too."

"Um, or not."

"What, why not? It will make the outfit super cute to turn them into a thick cuffed capri." She looked at me a second before understanding dawned on her face and she started laughing. At me. "Oh Lord, you still haven't shaved your legs, have you?"

"NO, of course I haven't. I am not a cheater so I'm not shaving my legs and I'm wearing my ugliest pair of granny panties that have holes in them and are saved for 'that time of the month' to protect my vow of not cheating."

Leah hugged me. "He must be something else to make you go to such lengths to make sure you don't accidentally end up naked."

"Girl, you have no idea."

"He's picking you up at six, right?" Leah looked at the clock. "You've got one hour. It's really nice out, not windy, so hair down. Pin back the sides if you feel uncomfortable with letting your freaky hair out. Makeup – keep it simple, nothing too heavy. Try to relax and enjoy yourself, maybe you'll at least get a great friend out of this." Another hug and she was out the door.

I rushed through hair and makeup and it seemed I had just laced up my sandals when I heard the doorbell ring. A quick check of the clock revealed that he was five minutes early. Sexy, sweet and punctual. I growled a little realizing that I really wished I was available to date him.

I opened the door and couldn't help but smile. Mark stood in front of me in an outfit that mirrored mine in its simplicity. T-shirt, jeans and leather thong sandals. He was holding his hand behind his back, smiled at me and brought his hand out showing a partially wilted bouquet of dandelions. I couldn't help but burst into laughing. All the nervousness I had about this not-date vanished immediately. He was playing it cool because he understood the situation.

With a renewed lightness that I hadn't felt in quite a while, I dropped a curtsy to him.

"Are those beautiful flowers for little ole me?" I was trying on a southern accent. I was failing. "Let me go put these in water." I took the sad little flowers and put them in an orange juice glass on my counter. Before I turned around I grabbed my phone and took a quick picture of them and shot out a text to my friends so they could see the flowers.

"Oh, the romance."

Giggling, I turned back for the door, and grabbed my purse on the way out.

"Your chariot awaits, milady." He offered his arm and laughing we walked down the path to his compact car. It was white, so I guess that would make him my white night.

"So where are you taking me?" I finally asked. I've never been accused of being patient.

"You'll see when we get there." Mark smiled at me. Grrrr.

"Did you just growl at me?"

Uh-oh. "Um, that was supposed to stay in my head."

"You're weird. I like weird."

We didn't talk much as we made our way to Onset, an awesome waterfront village that is a part of Wareham. I looked up when he parked and saw the name "Eatz" on the side of the building. I had heard about this restaurant but had never been. It was a newer place and specialized in local comfort food but with a twist.

I turned and grinned at him. I was thrilled with his choice.

"S'allright?" he asked.

"S'allright."

He walked over to my side of the car, opened the door for me, and reached for my hand as he helped me out of the car. Swoon! He offered his arm again, and so hand in arm we walked into the restaurant like we owned it. I was amazed at how awesome this place was. It had this super cool city vibe that was unusual out here on the coast.

Our conversation was minimal as we looked over the menu. I found a scallop and bacon flatbread. Scallops wrapped in bacon had always been a favorite, so I knew I had to give this a shot. After the waitress took our order we were left alone, and the silence was deafening. I had no idea how to get a conversation started. It was at that moment I realized I was on a date with someone who was pretty much a complete stranger.

I was racking my brain trying to think of a good ice breaking question. All I could come up with was "So, um, where are you from?"

Mark looked at me with a strange expression and then just started laughing.

"Really, that's the best you could come up with? You really are out of the game, aren't you?"

"Fine, Mr. Man of the Dating World. You think you can do better than that? Bring it." I leaned back in the chair and started to slowly drink my delicious margarita.

He had a sort of evil grin on his face as he watched me enjoy my drink and then leaned forward.

"So, how did you lose your virginity?"

The entire mouthful of margarita that I had left me and sprayed across the table. He had been anticipating it because when I opened my eyes he held a napkin up to block the spray.

He had a shit eating grin on his face as I coughed up margarita and God knows what.

"THAT'S your idea of an ice breaker?" I was incredulous. Who was he to ask me how I lost my virginity. I took a long, slow drink of my margarita. I started to feel warm. I started to feel a little tingly. And once the warmth over took me, and after I was overcome by his sexy as sin on a stick smirk, I started spilling my V-card revocation story.

"Okay, so here's the deal. I'll tell you my big virginity story. But you're gonna hafta tell me yours, too." So, this was the situation. I could hold my wine, but throw in a margarita and my jaw muscles were loosened and it was an Ashley Tell All.

He nodded, amused at how quickly I was caving.

"I was working in Rhode Island right out of high school. It was like working in a foreign land. It may have only been forty-five minutes away, but it was like another new, exotic land for me. After having been a pariah in junior and senior high school, I had found a group of people where I was accepted, I was…well…normal. They got my humor and the fact that I was fifteen to twenty years younger than them was no big deal. I was one of them. The one thing that was really weird was, with them so much older than me, they were able to have these inside sexual jokes that I really didn't get. I mean, I knew what they were alluding to because I read a lot. I mean, a lot. But I didn't really know what they were talking about. I'm still trying to figure out what they meant by the one-eyed turtle.

My mom terrified me about sex. Seriously terrified me. From the point when I turned thirteen until I was eighteen I heard that my first time would hurt, I wouldn't find satisfaction and I would more likely than not get pregnant. I heard that All. The. Damn. Time. So, I realized that if I was in a legit relationship, I might ruin it by being a virgin. Because I would be too terrified to get intimate with him, and if I did it would hurt and I'd end up pregnant.

There was this 'alternative lifestyle' magazine back then that was called 'Live RI'. In it were these personals. Personals you would not take home to mom. Some of them were pretty darned explicit. I picked one that didn't frighten the crap out of me, and called the mailbox number. I think I said something like 'Hi, my name is Ashley, and I'm a virgin...but I don't want to be anymore. I'm looking for someone to take care of that problem, but not want anything else. If you think that works for you, this is my number.' Shocker of all shockers, I got a call. Apparently, the lure of a virgin with no strings attached is something strong. We made arrangements for the following weekend.

I drove to his home, which was in Foxboro, in the shadow of Foxboro Sullivan Stadium. It was a trailer at Foxboro. Being a Pats fan, I felt it was some sort of freaky omen. Like the popping of my cherry was sanctioned by the New England Patriots, and thereby was completely acceptable.

I remember pulling up to his trailer, and when he suggested we go out for Chinese first I was conflicted. Part of me was a little touched that he wanted to help me feel less like a total whore by taking me out for dinner first. But the other part was all like, seriously? I'm a sure thing, let's get this done, take the V-card, and let me move on with my life.

We finally returned to his trailer, and things progressed as you would expect. I was more than a little surprised at how, well, small he was. I mean, I figured that the books I'd read were guilty of exaggeration; but this was ridiculous.

I remembered him trying to take care of me, you know, going 'down there'. And God, it did NOTHING for me. I mean, his breath was warm on my lady parts, and he was all whip-lash tongue on me. Then he started groaning and moaning all exaggerated. He kept looking up at me like I was supposed to be doing something. I finally caught on, he figured I should have been done already due to his Casanova-like ways. So, I summoned up everything I'd ever read, every movie I'd ever seen, and I faked the world's most spectacular orgasm."

Mark leaned forward like he was going to say something, but I held a hand up. "Wait, it gets better!"

"Once I sufficiently completed my 'performance', he sat back up on his heels, wiping his face. He had a cat who ate the canary grin on his face. He said to me, 'wow, I knew I was good, but I didn't realize I was that good.' I knew I must have looked confused, because he was quick to add, 'you just had a gusher!'

Considering that I had totally faked my orgasm, I was really confused as to what he meant. A gusher? No possible way. But then, I suddenly started to realize something. You see, I'd had a lot of water at dinner. I kind of had to pee when we started fooling around, but I just wanted to do the deed and get it over with that I didn't take the time to go to the bathroom. I reached below myself and sure enough, the sheets were wet. Oh, and I didn't really have to pee anymore.

It turns out that during my performance I accidentally peed. On his face. And he took it as something else and was so freaking proud of himself, he practically glowed.

I was mortified, but at the same time, inwardly laughing at the fact that I pissed all over him. He got a condom and finally completed the act, the whole reason I was there. I remember wondering how he found one so small, but realized that they must come in different sizes. It didn't hurt, I didn't bleed. So I figured that my mom was wrong all along.

Once it was all over, I thanked him, got dressed, and left as quickly as I could, laughing hysterically once I'd reached the highway."

Mark had tears rolling down his face. Because we were in a restaurant and all, he was trying to keep it in, but he was convulsing a little and had tears rolling down his face.

"A year and a half later, I had a boyfriend. I was his first. We were, um, intimate and it hurt. A-freaking-lot. When I went to the bathroom, there was blood. I suddenly realized what had happened. The guy who was my first, didn't 'break' me. I was technically still a virgin and was losing my virginity for the second time. I know you think I'm lying, but this really happened. I started laughing, hysterically. My poor, virgin boyfriend was in the bedroom hearing me laugh after his first time, and I heard him say, "um, Ashley..uh…is everything okay"? I realized that he got the wrong impression. I told him the whole virginity losing story, and at the end his reaction was that he felt so bad for the guy who wasn't big enough rock hard to take my virginity."

I sat back, my story complete. Mark finally gave in to the laughter, and was guffawing. I had to admit, my story was funny. I mean, seriously, you can't make this stuff up. The problem was that he was starting to attract the attention of the other guests at the restaurant. I looked around and smiled weakly, waving at them limply like the third runner up in a pageant.

"Pull yourself together! Okay, so, I told you mine, you have to tell me yours." I leaned forward, and rested my chin in my hands. I couldn't wait to hear what his story was.

"Geez, I'm kind of embarrassed after your story. I mean, that was epic."

"Hey, not cool. You spill your embarrassing little story and let me be the judge as to whether you deserve to stand in the presence of my epicness."

"Epicness? Is that even a word?"

"If it wasn't, it is now. Quit stalling and spill." I had no idea why I cared. I didn't even know if I really cared or not. But it was easier than sitting there and trying to figure out what the hell to talk about in this fake date I wasn't sure if I wanted to be on.

"Well, I was fifteen. My family and I were visiting a cousin in Texas. There was this really cute neighbor girl. Her family lived on the farm next door. She asked if I wanted to see the hay loft. Well, one thing led to another, and I lost it in a hay loft, in a barn, in Texas. Yeeeeee hawwwww!"

I started laughing at him, I mean, my story was better, no doubt. But losing it in a barn in Texas? That's one hell of a Texan souvenir.

"Wow, talk about cliché." I was still snickering at him a bit.

"Hey, whatever, I had a great time and I am pretty sure she did, too."

"Uh-huh, well, what was her name?"

He gave me the world's worst deer in the headlights look. "Uh... Brenda? Bobbi Sue? Briana? Crap, I can't remember. It's not like it was a relationship. It was just a roll in the hay."

We both looked at each other, and started laughing. That was just too bad not to laugh at.

After that, conversation came easy. The stress of date vs. non-date was over; so we just relaxed into it.

Mark looked at me after our dinner plates were cleared. "So, this guy you're kind of with, Craig, are you sure you want to still be with him?"

Ahhhh, the million dollar question. I wanted to answer 'of course' immediately, but I decided to actually think about it. Could I spend my life without Craig? Yes, I could. It would hurt, but I could do it. I would be fine. Did I want to spend my life without Craig? No. I missed his warm eyes. I missed the way his hair would never quite do what he wanted, and he inevitably would have a stray hair that looked like it was electrocuted. I missed that he didn't give a crap about fashion, and that he had, on more than one occasion, paired a plaid tie with a striped shirt (until I'd made him change it). Most of all, I missed that he seemed to get me, and accept me, and love me as I was. Well, until he didn't. I found myself getting sad as I realized what may have been lost.

I looked up and realized that while this inner dialogue was happening, Mark was sitting, patiently waiting for my answer.

"Yeah. I am positive I still want to be with him. I can't help but hope he finds his way back to me."

He nodded, a slow smile growing on his too sexy to be in public face. "Okay, then."

"Huh?"

"Listen, Ash, I think you are cute, funny and would probably be awesome girlfriend material. I have been trying to decide if you were really into your boyfriend or ready to move on. I'm not going to poach another guy's girl. So, even though there's a part of me that would love to try to be something more with you, I know it's not going to happen. That's fine. I think I'm okay, then, with being your friend."

"Ugh, do you have to be so damned perfect?"

"What?"

"Seriously, you are sexy as all sin, easy to talk to, funny, and you have those damned eye crinkles. Plus, you're somehow accepting of this mess that is my life right now and still want to be my friend?"

Mark started laughing at me. "I'm nowhere near perfect. At. All. I would be up for being your guy. But you aren't ready to shut the door on Craig, so that's not an option. You are a fun person to be around, being friends with you or not knowing you at all, I'll choose being friends with you."

Damned if the thought of friends with benefits didn't cross my mind and sound highly interesting at this moment. Dirty thoughts of the things we could do in the name of 'friendship' passed through my mind. I found myself licking my lips.

He raised an eyebrow at me. "Why you looking at me like a hot fudge and peanut butter sundae?"

"Uh, I'm not?" He just started laughing at me. Busted.

Suddenly, Leah's face popped into my mind. I pictured Leah and Mark together. His arm around her shoulders, smiling down at her with his blue eyes and sexy eye crinkles. I saw their marriage, and cute little Leah-Mark hybrid babies. Oh my gosh, they would be perfect for each other.

"Hey, would you like to go out next week?"

Mark looked really confused. "I thought you wanted to be with Craig?"

I started laughing. "Not me, crazy. My friend, Leah! You two would be positively perfect for each other."

"Ugh, a blind date? Seriously? I don't know, Ashley, blind dates are kind of a bad idea. I mean, there has to be a reason you need to set her up instead of her finding her own guys. Does she have a third nipple?"

"What, no, of course not. Well, I don't think she does."

"She into inflicting pain?

"Not that I've personally seen."

"Then why are you setting us up?"

"Because she's one of three best friends. She's gorgeous, funny, and she had a really, really bad dating experience a couple years ago. So she's sworn off men. But I think you guys would be awesome together. Please let me hook you guys up." I was bouncing up and down in my seat thinking of how to pull this off and help my friends find blissful coupledom.

"Ashley, you are taking a lot of liberties for a new friendship." I could tell he was trying hard to look stern, but his eyes were smiling at me. Swoon. NO, bad Ashley! No swooning over Leah's future husband and baby daddy.

I picked up my phone, and scrolled to a picture of the four of us taken a couple weeks ago. We may have been drinking too much wine. Scratch that. We were definitely drinking too much wine. I smiled at the memory of that day, the group karaoke, inappropriate girl-on-girl dancing, and teetering around like we weren't getting tipsy, even though we were already there.

I held out the picture to him, and pointed out Leah. "This, sir, is your mystery date."

He grabbed my phone, and held it closer. He zoomed in the photo and I saw his eyes darken a shade. If this was a romance novel, I would have written that his eyes darkened with desire.

"Okay. Next week. Same time, bring her here."

"Seriously? Oh my God, this is going to be incredible!" I grabbed my phone and sent Leah a text, telling her that this restaurant is awesome and that I was bringing her and the girls next week.

I then sent the girls a text saying that I was hooking up Leah with Mark and needed their help.

Mark grabbed my phone and read the texts. He finally looked up at me incredulously. "You're not telling her she's going on a date?"

"I told you, she had a bad dating experience and has sworn off men. If I tell her she's going on a date, she'll walk into with the enthusiasm of walking into a lion's den wearing the costume of a three month old lamb. You have to trust me. This is the only way it will work, and it will require some group trickery."

"Why am I starting to regret deciding that friendship with you would be a good idea?"

"Because you are realizing that you are wrong. It's a freaking great idea."

He just shook his head at me. "You're a mess." He said it with a smile, so I figured it wasn't a bad thing. I was already picking out my maid of honor dress. That's right, maid of honor. I'm the one who had the foresight to bring these two together, I get the honor. I was thinking that their first born should be named after me, too. I didn't think that was asking for too much.

I gave him my biggest grin. This was going to be so much fun.

Chapter 10

With a glass of red wine in hand, I sat down in my bedroom and started updating my blog with my dating adventures. I had to be very careful not to explain how Leah was soon to be dating Mark; because she was very good about reading my blog. I knew that I was going to have to type the details of the conversation we had, and I found myself laughing as I discussed his 'ice-breaker'. As shocked as I was when he brought it up, I had to admit that it did the job.

When I started laughing, Penny's head popped out from around the door. "Hey, girl." I set aside my laptop and waited for her.

"Mrowl!"

She came over and hopped onto my lap, kneading my leg as she started purring that beautiful, deep, wet purr. I heard a tiny little 'mrowl' and looked over to the door to see three kittens braving the big world outside of the closet, walking over to us in a little kitten line; with the tiniest one batting her big brother's tail. They couldn't figure out how to hop up, so one at a time I picked them up and laid them around their mom. Then it started, I heard the babies purring along with their mom. I rested my head against the wall, just totally wrapped up in that moment with my little family. I was pretty sure that listening to purring while I petted them all was more relaxing than any massage I'd ever experienced.

"No matter what comes of this blogging thing, I'm glad I did it. If I hadn't, I wouldn't have you guys."

Penny looked up at me, slowly blinking at me with what looked like a smile on her lips. She leaned over, gave Ressie, the orange kitten, a quick lick on the head. Then the little kitten started grooming herself. It was awkward, but super cute to watch. I sipped from the red wine in my glass and just enjoyed the moment.

My phone broke the silence of the moment and I glared at it. Even though I never turned the ringer up, it's vibrating was irritating because it killed my Zen. But I saw that Karyn's name was on the display.

"Hey, K, what's up?"

"Ash, I've got Alex here, can we come over? Gotta discuss the text you sent about next weekend."

"Yeah, c'mon over, I'm upstairs with the kittens."

What seemed like mere minutes later, I could hear the pound of their feet on the stairs. The cats heard them too, and they all dove for cover in the closet. I laughed at their bravery.

The girls came in and seemed surprised to see me curled up on the floor. Karyn raised an eyebrow at me.

"Just spending some time with my little family. Everyone grab a kitten, we're going downstairs and they're too little for the stairs."

We each went down the stairs with the kittens, a nervous mom following in our wake. We settled on the couch with some red wine, and let the kittens crawl all over us. Penny chose to sit in a chair where she could monitor us but at the same time get a little break from her kids. Not that I blame her.

Alex was the first to pipe up with questions about my master plan.

"So, you go on a hot date with Mark and you decided to hook him up with Leah? How did that happen?"

I laughed and told them about the date. Told them about the icebreaker and my response. They had all heard the story before, but it still put us in a fit of giggles. In case you ever wondered, hysteria and red wine do NOT go well together. So then I told them that he asked if I wanted to still be with Craig.

"I guess he was going to try for me, but after realizing that my heart was still tied to another man, he did the honorable thing and bowed out of the competition that wasn't. Knowing what we know about Leah and the less-than-honorable men she's had experience dating, I could see them working together as a couple. He's funny, and sexy, and sweet, and sexy, and patient…"

"And sexy…" Karyn and Alex chimed in. I laughed. "Did I mention he was sexy?"

"Only a couple times." Karyn said. "Hey, we've never seen a picture of how sexy he is. Do you have one?"

I picked up my phone and started scrolling through my album. "I may have secretly snapped one during class. Don't judge me."

The girls giggled at me as I handed over my phone. Alex pretend swooned over the side of my couch at the mere sight of him. Had this been a Victorian romance novel, I would have recommended that she loosen her stays.

"Are you sure you would choose Craig over Mark? I mean, dayum!" There was drool involved. Two grown women drooling over my fantasy come true was not something I felt comfortable about. I shook my head. I mean, two grown woman drooling over Leah's future husband was not something I felt comfortable about. Yeah, that's what I meant.

"How on earth are you going to get Leah to agree to go on a date with anyone, even if he is the double threat of both drool and swoon worthy? You know she's sworn off men since the Dylan disaster."

We all scowl at the mention of his name. That rat bastard played our girl for over a year. She thought they were on the road to holy matrimony, but it turned out that she wasn't the only one who felt that way. There were apparently at least four other women who also were convinced that Dylan was their forever. It had taken a while to bring regular smiles to Leah's face. It had been over two years.

"I'm not going to tell her she's going on a date. Because we are all going on a date." I cringed when I saw the shocked and somewhat disapproving looks shot my way by Alex and Karyn.

"You're ambushing her?"

"Not exactly...I mean, we're all going to go out together, and then if Mark is there, we will of course invite him over, it would be rude not to. We are not rude people."

"That's devious." I was expecting some level of disapproval, not the sinister smile that was creeping onto Alex's face.

We both looked at Karyn who seemed to have an internal fight going on in her mind. I found myself internally begging her to approve of the plan.

"Well, while I don't love the deception that you have planned, I miss seeing her really happy. I'd like someone to earn her trust who deserves to earn her trust. Are you sure that this Mark guy really is a good guy?"

"Everything I've seen about him shows he's a decent guy. I don't know him well enough to make any promises. He was cool to hang out with and seems to have a distaste for, as he put it, 'poaching'. Which is more than we can say for Dylan the Dick."

"So we go out to dinner, under the guise of you wanting us to experience this incredible restaurant you got to go to. He just happens to be there, we invite him over, and we enjoy each other's company?"

"Exactly. It will be a date, but only Mark and all of us know that. Leah will just think it's a coincidence. When we get ready to leave, I'm going to mention another restaurant I've been dying to try out. One of you will ask Mark to join us, as if he's an honorary part of the team. Slowly, over time, she'll come to trust him. When we all see that she's truly relaxed about him, we give the go-ahead to ask her on a legit date. One without us."

Karyn was bouncing up and down in her seat. I think I'd earned her support of this match making venture. Then again, she was about to get married so she was feeling the love thing.

"This is great! It lets them get to know each other in a safe, controlled environment where we can figure out how it's going and let it go to the next step or not." Karyn nailed it perfectly.

"Exactly. If they don't take to each other, no harm no foul. She'll never know we, um, meddled."

Alex looked at me a little strangely. "How would you feel if you found out we meddled in your love life and were pulling some puppet strings?"

My first reaction was that I would probably kill them. But I tried to imagine it, the emotions, and the thoughts that would go through my head if someone had tried to play puppet master with my love life. What I realized was, that as much as I would want to kill them, literally rip them apart limb from limb, I knew these lovely ladies. They had my back when the rest of the world seemed to turn its back. I knew they would always have my best interests at heart. So in the end, I'd probably silent treatment them for about a week and get over it.

"It would take some work but I'd get over it. After about a week. You know, the standard cool-off period."

Alex gave me a strange look, which was fleeting, and then nodded. "It's on."

We all squealed like it was third grade again and we were about to start chasing the cute boy around the playground. I had a quick moment of feeling bad for Leah. I turned and looked over my right shoulder, for some reason expecting Craig to be there. He wasn't. I was about to joke with him about this matchmaking plan. Suddenly, the high I was feeling over the fun I was having with my girls subsided a little. When would I stop looking, expecting to see him there? He's been gone now for over four weeks? I haven't heard a word except for the text telling me he was going away for work and would be in touch? When would I learn?

I felt my eyes well a bit. I shook it off, put on my best smile, and raised my glass. "I propose a toast to the future Mrs. Mark." We all laughed and then snuggled up to our kittens while Penny defiantly washed her butt in front of us. Life was good.

***

"So, they approve?" I looked up from the desk where I sat and saw familiar blue eyes.

I smiled at him. "Yeah, they are all aboard."

"How are you planning on this playing out? I'm not still one hundred percent sure I'm comfortable tricking your friend. I mean, you've already told me that she has trust issues with guys. Will she feel like I was a jerk for 'tricking' her into dating me by following your plan?"

Crap. That was a really good question. A really good question I hadn't begun to think about. All we worried about was how she would treat us after she found out. We didn't even begin to think about poor Mark. If I found out my friends had tricked me somehow in a relationship issue, would I also blame whatever guy was involved? Possibly. Okay, probably. I would figure he had more to do with this than they would.

"Mark, I am not going to do anything to thwart your future romance, marriage and little hybrids."

"Marriage and…hybrids? Are we talking about cars?" Poor guy looked so confused.

"No, silly, kids. Children. Babies. I'm talking little hybrids of you and my friend, Leah."

"Um, Ash, you think maybe you're getting a little ahead of yourself at all? I mean, right now, your friend knows my name, but nothing else about me. You are picking out china patterns and our children's names."

"You will name at least one after me. Maybe two. It's only right." I nodded at him as he stared at me in disbelief. "Hey, I'm bringing you two together, don't you think there should be some naming rights?"

"Holy crap. You might actually be psycho." Mark just looked at me, slowly shaking his head 'no' as he backed out of the room.

"You're still coming on Saturday, right?" I ran after him as he left the room.

"Yeah, sure."

That didn't give me many warm fuzzy feelings.

Maybe he was right. Maybe by pushing Leah into a situation where she would be forced to have a friendship with a guy, build up trust with a guy and hopefully – if my gut was right – get engaged to a guy would be wrong if under the wrong pretenses.

If I didn't know Leah's history, I might have caved and given in, letting her know everything. But she was so hurt, so burned by that assbag, Dylan, that as soon as she hears the words 'guy', 'date' or 'really nice ass' she shut down mentally. She was so shut off, that the only way we could handle this was to sneak a hottie into her life. I remembered how she was looking sort of sad talking about him as I was getting ready. I thought she might be getting ready, mentally, to entertain the thought of a guy being a part of her life.

"Mark, she's ready. She doesn't know she's ready, but she's ready. She's been through so much, and is not going to trust quickly. But once she gives her heart, it's yours. You'll have to earn it on your own. But I think you've got it. The question I have, is whether you are willing to put so much on the line for a chick you've never met."

Mark's eyes turned dark again, like they did when they looked at her photo. He looked down at his hands while he carefully chose the words he would say. As he looked up, I felt as if I had been punched in the stomach by the look of raw pain on his face.

"When you showed me the picture of your friend on your phone, my first reaction was how pretty she was. The second thought was how beautiful her smile was. The third thought was the fact that her smile never quite reached her eyes in that picture. I wanted to know how such a beautiful woman could smile with so much pain in her eyes. I would like to get to know her, find out about her. With her approval, I'd like to maybe be her person. I do not, however, want to be the reason that any more pain reaches those gorgeous eyes."

I was quiet. I could not speak. If I tried, my voice would break. He'd never met her. Until Saturday, he'd not even known her name. Yet, he spoke about her with more insight than her closest friends had. When was the last time I'd seen the sadness in her eyes? I didn't even remember. Yet he, a complete stranger, looked at a picture of a somewhat tipsy night and didn't just see a beautiful girl. He looked at a picture and saw pain. He saw hurt. We all thought that she'd healed and was better. I guess we'd seen what we wanted to see. He saw someone who he wanted to help. In that moment, I was certain that I'd chosen the right person for her.

"You are right for her. You are too good for me. However, you are all sorts of perfect for my Leah." I squeezed his hand as I stood up and walked out of the room. I stopped short of the door and turned to look at him over my shoulder.

"I know you two will be fabulous together, however, I have to ask you... will you fight for what you believe in? She's not going to give in easily, and I need to know that you don't give up easily. It will take a lot to get her to trust again."

He glared at me a little before answering.

"If after getting to know her I decide she's the woman I've been waiting for, and only then, I guarantee, a million armies couldn't stop me from standing by her side."

My voice cracked as I said, "That's all I could ask for."

Once I got to the car, I wrote down everything I remembered him saying. The girls needed to hear this. Karyn who wasn't one hundred percent certain at first, specifically. She needed to know the crazy level of understanding that Mark had for our Leah. I didn't want to miss a syllable. I was so enamored with this potential coupling I considered to be fated in the stars that I was close to buying her some glass slippers and making her sleep in the fireplace.

I sent out a text with all the details to Alex and Karyn. I waited. I knew that it would be little to no time before my phone would vibrate in excitement with their response. My patience paid off.

"OMG, my panties are wet."

Geez, guess who.

"Alex, crude, much?"

"What? He sounds like the perfect male which makes me think he'd prefer dudes over boobs. But I'm not one to judge."

"Bull... you totally are the one to judge." I disagreed with her in less than a heartbeat.

"Okay, so maybe I will judge a teensy bit, but it's because I love. However, if the teech said even a quarter of what you are telling us, I will drug her, bind and gag her, and place her on his bed with a ginormous red velvet bow covering her best parts."

Was Alex jealous that I was pairing Mark with Leah? I hadn't really ever given much thought to whether Alex was happy being single or not. She was always so tough and strong and snarky. I started feeling that twisting in my stomach again. Maybe I was wrong. Maybe he wasn't supposed to be Leah's. What if he should have been paired with Alex? I squinted, trying to picture him and Alex. What I imagined in my head was her straddling his back while wearing a pair of spurs. I saw a spanking so hard that his left butt cheek had her hand permanently bruised in his white flesh. I shuddered, Alex was so not his person. She would break that poor man!

I couldn't even begin to picture Leah with a whip, let alone leather chaps and a riding crop. I had a feeling the two of them would be a perfectly loving, normal couple. Mark and Alex were not a good idea, but I was pretty sure that there was someone out there that could handle her without taming her.

***

I was still riding pretty high from my conversation with Mark and my realization that I was very possibly the best match maker in the entire universe when I got home. When I got to the side door of the house I was juggling my backpack, my purse, my water bottle, my cell phone and my car keys while digging in my purse for my house keys. Yes, I kept my home and car keys on separate key rings. In the midst of my impressive juggling performance I realized that there was an envelope closed in my door. I was a little confused because the only person who ever did that was the propane guy, and he didn't darken my doorstep in the summer.

I glared at the offending piece of paper, and because my hands were full I had to basically grab it with my mouth. First world problems, right there. The struggle was real.

When I finally got through the door I dumped everything on the kitchen table and spat the envelope out on my counter. My name was typed on it, not handwritten so I had no idea what was in it. That seemed strange to me.

My mind immediately went to a crime drama. What if this was some sort of crazy ransom note, and my family members were being held hostage? What if when I opened the letter, it was written using clippings from all sorts of different magazines and newspapers? I put my hand to my mouth. I could have compromised evidence by putting the envelope in my mouth and getting my DNA filled saliva on the envelope. Or what if it was laced with some form of a narcotic, or some arsenic or anthrax? Did I taste something funny? I thought maybe I tasted something funny. It was entirely possible that my tongue was going numb.

My overactive imagination was kicking into overdrive, and I had to mentally restrain myself from going and brushing my teeth in hopes of diluting the effects of the mysterious drug that I had imagined to be present on the envelope.

I decided I was being a total idiot, so I just laughed at myself, took the envelope and opened it up. I unfolded the papers that were in there. Registration confirmation. Huh? What had I registered for? I went through my mental file of all my activities for the past few days and I didn't remember a single thing I'd registered for. I focused my attention back on the piece of paper, and as I kept reading I saw that I had apparently registered four people for a pole dancing class at Pole Diva Dance in Plymouth on Friday night. What on Earth had I been drinking that I registered a group of people for pole dancing? I was the least rhythmic person I knew.

During a summer program when I was in junior high I was part of a flag twirling group. It was just something fun we did for an end of season talent show. I kept having to be told to stop being so 'militant' in how I twirled my flag, that it wasn't supposed to be sharp and crisp but fluid. I couldn't quite get the hang of it, so I was put to the back row. It was the same as when I was three and in ballet, I was put at the back of the stage.

I was told that it was because I was the tallest. I took a lot of pride believing that I was the tallest, and therefore somewhat special. They didn't just put me in the back row, they put me in the back row and in the middle. Honestly, I was so well hidden from view that my parents couldn't even find me.

I'm not kidding. Mom and Dad came clean a few years ago as we were looking at family photos and I pointed to myself. They then, very sheepishly, admitted that wasn't me. Apparently the night of the recital, they couldn't find me. They were sitting towards the right hand side, and there were taller girls in front of me. So they just started clicking off picture after picture, figuring at some point they'd get me in the frame. After the photos were printed, they took out a magnifying glass. It took over an hour for my mom to find a wisp of my hair behind a girl. That was the only evidence that I took ballet. I grew up believing that I was the girl who was the second from the right. Mom and dad said that was me, so I believed it. What I took away from this experience is that the back row is not just where the extra special tall kids go. That was where the less than talented kids went.

Pole dancing, though? What the hell was I thinking?

I looked back down and saw that it a gift from 'The Girls'. I was going to have to kill them. I guess I was saying that a lot these days. Their days were clearly numbered. It was signed all three of them, so I didn't even know who was the responsible party.

Pole dancing. UGH. I could barely walk down the stairs without stumbling and getting injured. I obviously couldn't walk in high heels without taking myself out, a bench out and potential innocent bystanders out. If this was a registration for four, that must mean they are taking the class, too. Good. Let's see how they do in this humiliating experiment.

Wait a minute. If they were there, that meant there would be witnesses. I pulled out my phone and wrote a quick group text.

'You're all dead to me. There will be no cameras allowed.'

I went upstairs to get changed into my sexy jammies. Oh, and by 'sexy jammies', I mean a pair of yoga pants and a loose t-shirt. When I walked into my bedroom I was overcome by the level of stank that hit me. What the hell happened in here? I looked at the walls and was surprised to find that the paint was not peeling. Wondering if one of the cats had died I peeked into the closet and started gagging. Oh dear Lord in Heaven. I couldn't breathe! My eyes were watering so bad that it made my mascara run a little, which meant that the mascara went into my eyes causing them to sting. I was walking blindly in the bedroom, unable to see for the tears and pain in my eyes. I walked straight into one of the posts of my four post bed. Freakin' OW! A very creative string of curse words flew from my mouth as I'd managed to stub my little toe as well as jam my nose on the post. I imagined a sailor looking at me in abject horror over my creative use of questionable language. Then I imagined a whole string of soldiers covering their ears.

Hmmmm, a string of soldiers. Yummy. Argh! I needed to get my head out of the gutter. I groaned and made my way gingerly to the bathroom and splashed water on my face, and used a wet facecloth to wash the mascara out of my eyes. I went back to the closet holding the facecloth over my face and nose and saw that the closet, which had been nice and clean this morning, was a disaster of kitty litter, blankets and a worn out looking momma kitty. There was litter everywhere. Some in the food dish, some in the water dish, a lot on the floor. The litter box. Oh, the litter box. It appears my little kittens had discovered how to use it.

Mental note, get a bigger box, or two. I ran downstairs to grab the trash barrel from the kitchen, as well as the vacuum and set about to cleaning up the mess.

I decided that if the kittens were old enough to use the box, they were old enough to come out of the closet. I moved the litter box to the bathroom, making sure the feline family got to see where it was so they wouldn't think this meant that my house was potty time free-for-all. I opened a window and shook out their blankets. After scooping up an armful of kittens, I went downstairs and settled on the couch. Penny followed closely and joined us. She hoisted up her hind leg and started bathing an area of her body that I would never, ever lick. Especially after seeing how nasty that litter box was. Blyech! The kittens were trying to copy their mom, which was hysterical. Little Midnight attempted the leg hoist but did it a little too ambitiously, and flopped right over on his back.

Penny was so flexible, though, I figured maybe I should send her to the pole dancing class in my place. A mental image of Penny swinging around a pole upside down went through my head, which started a fit of giggles, which shot some wine out my nose. Have you ever laughed so hard wine came out your nose? It's not fun. It's also not the first time that had happened. I was an exceptional level of special.

See, that level of gracefulness was the proof that in no way should I ever be allowed in a room that had a stripper pole. Or mirrors. I shouldn't be allowed in the same block as that building.

I opened up my laptop and searched for Pole Divas Dance, the name of the studio where I would be going for humiliation this Friday night. Front and center on their page there was a woman, upside down, legs spread out, holding on to the pole with her two hands. That was all that was supporting her, her two hands. Oh, and she was smiling at the camera. Freakin nut. I scrolled through all of their photos, and then there were the videos. I was dying watching these. What in the hell were my friends thinking signing me up for this class? I started to wonder if they were picking their 'assignments' for me every week by trying to determine how to humiliate me just a little bit more than the person did the week before.

I clicked on another video and my jaw dropped as this girl took a running leap at the pole, with her legs spread wide open. When she made contact with the pole, her arms and legs wrapped around it, then she let go with her arms, swirling around the pole with only her legs holding on. Not only was I madly impressed with this woman's leg strength, I was surprised that her vag wasn't bruised and battered from the number of times she had to practice that move. I mean, seriously. It wasn't as if the first time she took a running leap towards a metal pole her legs did the perfect grab and swing. I wondered if a woman's holiest of holies kept taking a blunt force trauma beating, would it start to go numb? Or worse, would there be such drastic nerve damage that the poor woman wouldn't be able to feel a damned thing that was going on down below.

I was trying to imagine what it would be like if my parts were as numb as my mouth after a dentist's visit. You know what it's like, when you can't feel the side of your face, so you start slapping your cheek to see if you can feel it? Imagine if you were slapping your mound as hard as you cold, just trying to feel anything, but you felt nothing? Oh even worse, if your significant other was …down there… and was clocking some serious overtime trying to get even the smallest reaction, but because of your pole dancing injuries you're yawning and falling asleep. Jeez, how would I explain that to the Emergency Room attending physician?

The horror of these possible scenarios had me picking up my phone and send one more group text.

"If I repeatedly slam into the pole and suffer permanent nerve damage in the girly zone, I'm never talking to you again."

This was going to be a long week.

Chapter 11

Do you know what you should not do if you are nervous about something? You should not watch every video known to man about the topic. I watched pole dances from professionals, from amateurs and from everything in between. I found a video on the internet that had a pleasantly plump woman attack the pole that she set up in her house, it fell over, and she crashed through her coffee table to the floor. Sex game, over. Every video I could find about fitness pole dancing showed women working out in something slightly less than a pair of booty shorts and a tank top. Seriously? Me wearing booty shorts would not make the world a better place. I found myself fascinated by the outfits and the 'dance' moves. I mean, how on earth did they do splits upside down and then scissor around the pole and not end up with that flimsy piece of material they called 'clothing' permanently become a part of their ass crack?

Friday night arrived and I found myself looking not nearly as sexy as the chicks in the video wearing a pair of yoga pants, a sports bra and a t-shirt over the sports bra. Yes, I fully understood that the pole dance outfit I was wearing was exactly the same as my 'relax at home and time for bed' outfit. I stopped where the GPS brought me and was surprised. Instead of having a sign out front that said 'GIRLS GIRLS GIRLS' it looked like a normal store front with big curtains in the front windows so you couldn't see what was going on inside.

I walked inside and was thrilled I wasn't the first person in the class to arrive. I've always had this weird knack of being the first person to arrive for everything. Parties, conferences, half naked exercise classes…I'll be there first.

My first impression was…loud. Loud, thumping bass house music that your hips can't help but move to, even if it's less than rhythmic. I may have looked like I was having a seizure. There were no videos, and therefore no proof.

A five foot two bundle of energy bounced over to me. I wasn't kidding. She literally bounced.

"Hi, my name is Sierra. What's your name?"

"Uh, Ashley?"

"OHMYGOD!! You're one of my newbs. I'm so excited, I love teaching this class, it's so much better than when I was dancing for money, ya know!"

My jaw dropped. Seriously hit the floor. I thought this was a professionally led class, not a stripper led class.

All of a sudden, Sierra's face broke into the biggest grin and she was bent over laughing at me. But the laughter wasn't just coming from her. I look around the room and I realize that all of them were smirking or hiding laughter from me.

"That never gets old!" Sierra was trying to catch her breath. "Okay, so I'm not a stripper, former stripper or aspiring stripper. I've been a personal trainer, semi-professional ballet dancer and fitness instructor for the past seven years. Consider yourself pole-hazed."

Again, there was more snickering from the rest of the group. I looked around the room, expecting a bunch of scantily clad women who were so skinny that they would fit into a pair of jeans made for five year olds. What I saw was one woman who was (Lord, don't strike me down) a little chunky, one who was older than my mother, and someone who looked younger than me but painfully shy. Shoot, if these were my classmates, I could totally do this. I mean, seriously, if a seventy year old retiree could swing around a pole, I certainly could.

Right about the time my chest started puffing out thinking that I was going to be the star of the class, I heard a commotion from the front door. In walked the divas. Alex, Leah and Karyn sashayed…I'm not exaggerating, they sashayed into the room. I slapped my hand over my face at Alex's outfit. She was wearing a sparkly sports bra and booty shorts. I was being really generous in calling them shorts. If booty shorts and bikini bottoms met, fell in love, and had a baby…that's what she was wearing. Oh. And fishnets. She wore fishnets to our first pole dancing class.

Leah and Karyn were much more subdued, but still wore shorts and a tank. I looked down at my yoga pant, sports bra and t-shirt. I looked around the class and realized that everyone looked more like Leah and Karyn. Sierra was dressed more like Alex. I was the most covered person in this class. I might as well have been wearing a muumuu.

The girls stopped and stared at me as if I was naked.

"What in the hell are you wearing?" Alex put a fist to her hips and glared at me, actually glared at me.

"Uh, yoga pants? A t-shirt?" I couldn't understand why she was going ape over my outfit. I mean, hello, it wasn't as if we hadn't already discussed my lack of fashion ad nauseam. "What's the big deal?"

"Did you even bother to read the registration form?"

I looked at her with a bit of confusion. No, of course I hadn't. I'd seen the words 'pole dance' and pretty much blanked out everything else.

I had the registration form in my purse, so I went over to quickly scan it. My heart sank when I saw below the actual registration information:

"To get the most benefit from this class, and to best grip the pole, we highly recommend wearing a tank top and a pair of shorts."

I looked up and saw myself in the mirror, tilting my head I took in my outfit. Long pair of yoga pants, a t-shirt that was very loose with longer sleeves than normal. I looked around the room and realized the rest of the women there were wearing sleeveless tops and shorts. Not necessarily the butt-floss shorts that Alex wore, but shorts, nonetheless.

"Seriously, this is my first class. I doubt I'll be swinging upside down from the pole today. I'm sure I'll be fine." I huffed, striding over to my pole. Yes, I chose the pole in the very back corner of the class. What's your point? Remember, I was one of the tall girls.

"Okay, everyone. We're going to start out by stretching. Put both hands on your pole, feet at the pole and butt out, flat back. You're stretching your arms, your shoulders and your hamstrings." Sierra bounced to the front, leading us through a litany of stretches. I was a little annoyed. I'd sort of hoped we'd get right to the nasty stuff. I mean, I wasn't any level of coordinated, but I didn't come here to get a good stretch. I'd actually done one of my yoga DVD's before I came here so that I'd be all limber and stretchy for the class.

"Now that we're all loosey goosey, let's review the moves we've been working on."

Wait, what we'd been working on? I hadn't worked on shit! I looked at the girls with panic in my eyes. I thought this was a beginner class. None of them would meet my eyes. They knew. They freaking knew that this was NOT a beginner class and they still signed me up. I was seriously starting to think that they were trying to hurt me. Mental note: look to see if a life insurance policy had been taken out on me.

"We were working on the fireman last week, so let's review. You're gonna start by putting your dominate hand on the pole like your gripping a baseball bat. So if you're right handed, use your right hand. Reach that hand as high as you can. Oh, and remember, lean away from the pole. You want all your weight to be on the exterior of the spin, that's what give you the momentum you need. That's right, Gram, looking good."

Gram? The older woman was her grandmother? I mentally raised a glass to the woman that was light years cooler than I would ever be.

"Now, leading with your dominant side foot, step, step, step; then swing your non-dominate leg out and around the pole. Pull your other leg up and swing around as you descend to the floor. Don't forget to bring your non-dominant hand to the pole at ninety degrees to your body, also in a fireman's grip. That will help you keep your body weight away from the pole so you don't go spinning into it."

Around the room I heard giggles and happy squeals as everyone swirled around the pole like they'd been doing it for years. Me, well, I was struggling with the basic instructions. Okay, dominant hand. So that meant my right hand. I grabbed the pole with my right hand. I strode around the pole, putting on my best stripper swagger. I had started with the wrong foot, though, and managed to get my legs tangled up. I never even quite got the leg to swing around the pole. Crap.

Take two, and I swung the right foot around, but because of my uninspired wardrobe choices, there was no grip and instead of swinging around the pole gracefully, my legs slid down and I was hanging by one arm, until that gave and I ended in a cross-legged heap at the bottom of the pole. I looked to my right, and was Alex, practically humping the pole. Karyn and Leah were both working at being perfectionist pole dancers. Near perfect form, the two of them. I wouldn't have been surprised if they were trying to out pole-dance each other. I stood up, dusted myself off, grabbed the pole in a baseball grip (seriously, what the hell was that?), took three uuber sexy strut walks, swung my left leg out, wrapped it around the pole and slid down. Damn yoga pants.

I'd mentioned before that I hated admitting when I was wrong. Hated. It. But I had to admit I was wrong in wearing the yoga pants. I bent over, and cuffed the pants as high as I could. So instead of being extra-long, bell bottomed yoga pants, they were black shorts that came above my knee and had a cuff about two inches thick. I looked like I was wearing some form of 1930's bloomers. I tried to strut back to my pole, but with two inch thick cuffs on each side I was walking like I had the stripper pole shoved up me.

With determination I gripped the hell out of the pole, walked with purpose for exactly three steps. Then I catapulted my left leg around that pole with strength I didn't know I had. I spun around the pole, and at the speed I went I actually heard a squeaking noise as my thigh...my poor, poor thigh, was smooshed against the pole and being pulled around it.

When I was a kid we did a horrifically politically incorrect thing called an 'Indian sunburn'. It was when you took someone's arm with both your hands, and pulled the skin in opposite directions. I'm pretty sure my pole dancing attempts created an Indian sunburn of epic proportions on my thighs. Tears were pouring down my face as I managed to complete the maneuver.

We kept practicing this move for about five minutes. It felt like thirty. I was pretty sure it was at least thirty minutes, maybe an hour. I was afraid to look at my thighs and calves. I was pretty sure I had no skin left.

I thought once I'd swung my happy ass around the damned pole that we would all call it a day. Oh, hell no.

"Great job, ladies. You are doing a great fireman. Let's move on to the V-spin." At Sierra's announcement, cheers went up around the room. I looked at my friends with panic in my eyes. They both grinned back at me. I got the distinct impression they knew what this was.

"So you're going to start with your dominant hand in a baseball grip high above your head. Then you're going to do your three sexy steps on tippy toes like in the fireman. This time, when you go for the spin, you are going to face the pole and put your other hand on the bottom of the pole in a reverse baseball grip. Both legs up, parallel to the floor in a 'V' shape, and swing around as you gracefully descend the pole. Like this."

She showed us how to do the V-spin with each step really exaggerated, then again quickly so we could see how it really looked.

I looked around the room, everyone was doing it with no problems. Gram hopped on that pole like she'd been working it since the Prohibition Era. If Gram could do it, I was certain that I could.

I put my right arm up and gripped that pole in what Sierra called a baseball grip. On my toes I counted out one, two, three; I turned toward the pole and went to reach for it with my other hand and that is when everything got out of control. I had my upper hand too high up on the pole so when I put my left hand on at waist level it pushed my face towards the pole. I cracked my forehead on the pole which made me let go with my right hand. I fell backwards, while still holding on with my left and then WHAM! Lady bits into the pole. UGH. I slowly, not so gracefully slid down the pole until my back was on the ground, my hand was between my legs still holding onto the pole and my legs were up in the air.

What was it with these crazy friends of mine that all of our adventures ended with me on my back and my legs in the air? I could think of a million much more fun things that involved me on my back with my legs up. I opened my eyes to five faces peering down at me. This was such de ja vu.

"Wow, look who skipped beginner and went straight to inversion." That was Gram. Gee, thanks, Gram. I let my legs fall to the ground, and used the pole to stand up.

"Guys, I'm going to give my lower regions a little break." I tried to walk over to the corner seats normally. Judging by the snickering around me I was not successful. I looked up at the mirror and saw that I was walking like I'd just ridden a horse for about five hours. A really fat horse. Groan.

"Okay, everyone, let's kick this up a notch! Enough beginner review."

With that, the music go louder, the hips swung a little further and suddenly I was at a strip club watching these ladies work the pole. Even Gram. Especially Gram. She started shimmying her replaced hips and shaking her maracas. I was impressed that she could, because gravity had long since set in, and it was no small feat for her to shake what her Mama gave her. Everyone looked like they were having so much fun. I was honestly having a blast watching them. I decided I would come back, but I would come back for beginner classes.

"Inversion time!" Sierra went over the steps with everyone on how to safely get upside down, then went pole to pole to walk them through the steps. She checked one everyone except her grandmother. I felt ashamed watching a woman who was thirty or forty years older than me flip upside down, then right herself. When she got to the ground she added a hip thrust and then shook her girls some more like a boss. It was decided. I wanted to be her in thirty years. Oh hell, who was I kidding…? I wanted to be her now.

After Sierra was convinced that everyone could get there on their own she bounced over to the MP3 player and selected a song. I squealed when I heard the first few strains of 'Pour Some Sugar on Me'. Oh man, my guilty pleasure song. The women started stalking their poles, and walked around them with professional level determination. I went back to my pole and at least did the beginner moves (which I did much better this time). When it got time for the inversion tricks I ran to my purse and grabbed some ones, running around the room, making it 'rain'. With the last strains of the song we all collapsed in giggles on the floor.

"Okay, okay everyone." Poor Sierra was gasping for air. "Thank you so much for coming to Intermediate Pole. Please check our website for more classes and times if you would like to learn more. To see videos of today's session, please go to the secure section of the website. If you already have video access great, you'll need to see me for log in access.

Wait, video? Oh, shit. I turned and glared at Alex, Leah and Karyn. They laughed at me. I told them no cameras, but even I knew that they'd found the perfect loophole. I rolled my eyes, went to the front and asked for my log-in access. Truth was, I wanted to see it. I knew I'd look ridiculous, but for some reason, I didn't care. I hadn't laughed this much in a long time.

Sierra smiled at me as she handed it over. "Did you have a good time?"

"Oh my gosh, yes! Do you have beginner classes? Ones where I can learn the basics a little slower and perhaps with less vaginal bruising?"

She laughed. "Yes, of course I do. I was wondering how you got signed up for intermediate." I pointed at the three musketeers. "Ahhhh, makes perfect sense. I teach a beginner classes on Mondays at six." My face fell a little.

"Oh man, I won't be able to start for a few weeks, I'm doing a blogging class that still has a couple weeks left."

She smiled. "I can always do one on one."

"That would be great, the less public humiliation I get, the better." We laughed, and agreed on Sunday afternoon around 1:00pm. We exchanged phone numbers so that we could get in touch with each other

I looked at the guilty parties, linked my arms with Leah and Karyn (Alex was on the end) and said, "Okay you crazy bitches, let's go get some ice cream." I turned and looked at our pole dance instructor. I thought for only a second and said, "You coming, Sierra?" I knew I'd made the right choice when her face lit up with the first real smile I'd seen on her since we walked. In. Oh, man, that girl had a story and a half. I wondered how long it would take for us to hear it.

Leah, Karyn and Alex looked at me in shock. They were always a little more open to new people than I was. What can I say? I was your classic New Englander. I wasn't necessarily cold to people, but I needed to get to know someone first before I wanted to spend any time with them. So I knew why they were looking at me like an alien being. Sierra linked arms with Alex and off we went. Okay, so we got stuck in the doorway and had to unlink arms a bit, but you get the idea.

***

The next morning I sat up and bed and yawned. Little blue birds flew in through the window, landed on my headboard and sang to me. A unicorn galloped through the bedroom, farting sparkles along his path. Okay, so that was total bull. What really happened was I tried to sit up. I tried to sit up about four times. Apparently my 'sitting up' muscles were on hiatus. I pulled the covers back and found that my arm muscles were also on strike. Either that or they hated me. Lots of hate. I somehow managed to scoot over to the side of the bed and slowly put one leg at a time on the floor.

Standing up I went to take the first step and almost fell to the ground. Small tears squeezed out of my eyes as I willed my muscles to work for me, not against me. I stiff legged it to my bathroom, where I realized I really had to 'go' and was terrified about the process of lowering myself down. I tried to get into a sit position but to no avail. Finally, I put one hand on my sink vanity and another on the back of the toilet as I slowly lowered myself down, walking my feet out at the same time. I sat down and whimpered.

I finished up and stiff walked to the top of the stairs. Looking down the stairs I was shocked to find out that where I used to have fifteen stairs on this staircase, I had somehow overnight gone to over one hundred stairs. Walking down looked like the impossible task. So I grabbed a hold of the railing and slowly lowered myself to the ground. Yes, I slid down the stairs on my butt. No, I was not ashamed. Yes, I really was. A little. When I got to the kitchen to turn on the coffee machine, I realized that I had a text message on my phone. Who on earth was texting this early in the morning?

I took my cup of coffee, and my phone and went to the living room. I pulled out my laptop and logged into Sierra's video website to see the videos of last night's class. That's when I realized that there were separate cameras for each girl. I watched my video, and was laughing so hard there may or may not be a small wet spot on my couch. Oh Lord, it hurt so much to laugh. Hurt. So. Much. I saved the video to my computer. That was so going on the blog. I stopped myself for a second. When did this happen? When did I go from hating the thought of people laughing at my expense and feeling humiliated to leading the charge? When did I stop taking it all too seriously? Huh.

Too much introspection with too little wine. I picked up my phone and checked out the text message. Turns out it had been sent last night, not this morning.

"Hey, Ashley, you may want to drink a little extra water tonight, your muscles may be sore tomorrow."

Huh, ya think? She really was very sweet. I'm sorry I called her an obnoxious bobble headed Barbie Doll. Maybe I didn't call her that to her face, but I totally called her that in my head. Especially when she was upside down on that pole making it look like a beginner move.

Looking again at the video on my computer I got a brilliant idea. A wonderfully horrible, brilliant idea.

"Thanks, girl. Just got this today. Owwwwww. Hey, can you do me a favor? I kind of want to get back at the girls for some of the things they've put me through lately. Just harmless fun, but it's time for me to get back. Can I have their video codes?"

My phone rang a heartbeat later.

"What on Earth did they do to you?"

I sat back and smiled. I know I could be annoyed at some of the things that had happened as a result of a slightly tipsy evening several weeks ago. But the truth is, I hadn't had the time to focus on the pain of maybe losing Craig, and I've actually –dare I say it – I've actually had fun going on these 'adventures' with my friends. I filled my new friend on everything. Craig needing a 'break', blogging, hot instructors, kittens and high heels. She was laughing so hard she was gasping for air.

"Oh my gawd, I would have killed them!"

"I keep threatening."

"Okay, okay, I'll text you the info for the videos. You didn't get it from me, though."

I assured her I would not reveal my source, but let's face it, my friends weren't dumb. I didn't care, this was going to be hysterical.

My phone beeped with the text giving me the information I needed. Giggling, I logged back in to the website and saved the videos I needed to my computer. I looked at the clock and realized I had less than an hour to make it to the coffee shop for our weekly meeting. I groaned as I hoisted myself up off of the couch and made it upstairs to get cleaned up. Making it up the thousands of stairs that I suddenly had took a bit.

I was only about five minutes late, not bad considering the injuries I had sustained. We had a great time as always, gabbing on about everything and nothing at all. I had to keep my internal smile to a minimum. I was glad to see that I wasn't the only one suffering from oddly sore muscles in odd places. I had actually seen a bruise on my upper inner thigh. I figured that must have been when I was doing the V-spin. Okay, maybe claiming that I had successfully completed the V-spin is a bit disingenuous. We started discussing our aches and pains like a bunch of old ladies at the nursing home.

Later that afternoon I finally did it. I logged into my Facebook account and posted each girl's video on their respective pages. Then sat back enjoying the sounds of my phone pinging with every 'like' and comment. I waited, though, for what I knew was coming once the girls saw the videos themselves.

I waited.

And waited.

Geez, what was taking them so long? I started to get nervous. Oh my God, what if they were driving when the video came across on their phones, and then in shock they'd driven straight into a tree? What if they were lying in a ditch dying somewhere?

My doorbell rang and I got up to see who was there. I looked out the window and saw three somewhat annoyed looking females. Whew, not dead in a ditch. Pissed on my doorstep, instead. That's a good thing. Kind of.

I opened the door, grinning from ear to ear knowing I'd gotten them.

All three stepped through at the same time, index fingers pointing me in the chest.

"BITCH!" They all yelled at me, in unison, which was funny as hell and belied the stern looks on their faces. We all stared at each other for a few moments before collapsing in giggles.

"C'mon in, let's get the wine going."

The girls went into the living room, each picking a kitten to cuddle. The kittens, of course, were more than happy to oblige. Penny joined me on the couch, finding a place where she could observe her babies but at the same time enjoy a little piece and quiet for a change.

Alex held up the one I called Rescue. "I like this one, she's got crazy red hair like you." You could hear the kitten purring from across the room. Penny looked at her kitten, then at me and said "Mrowl!" Damned if I didn't think she was agreeing with Alex.

"So, awesome move posting the pole dancing videos on Facebook. We deserved that after putting you in an intermediate class." Leah grinned at me from behind the kitten she was holding up as a shield.

"First, thanks, I appreciate the recognition of my awesome brilliance." I ignored the snort of laughter coming from Alex. "Second, do you really think that Callie can protect you? Sad."

"How did you get those videos? Karyn was dangling her hoodie cord over Midnight, who thought it was about the most fun in the world to bat at it.

"I shan't reveal my sources." I mustered up my snootiest voice, sticking my nose firmly in the air. More laughter from the room.

"I figure it had to be Sierra, which means she's fair game." Alex grinned, I could see those wheels turning in her head as she tried to decide what the best form of revenge would be. She was a brilliant evil mastermind. I was more than a little frightened at how that girl's mind worked sometimes.

"Sierra is an innocent party in all dealings. I like her, guys, how did you find her?"

"I started taking pole dancing classes a few months ago. I thought that Chris might enjoy the results. I mean, I really wanted to be able to do a seductive dance for him without looking like a complete idiot." Karyn admitted to us, looking a little shy. "I started really enjoying myself, so I kept going to classes. Sierra and I really hit it off, I figured you guys would love her. She comes off as Bimbo Barbie at first, but once you get to know her you realize there is a LOT more there."

"How could you possibly have ever called her Bimbo Barbie?" I asked in mock horror. Karyn hung her head in shame. "I at least added 'bobble head' in my mental description." She looked up at me in shock, surprised that I would be so cold to someone I hadn't met. I put my hands up in front of me in defense. "Dude, she bounced over to me in booty shorts and a sports bra. She bounced! I have no mental defense against attacks like that."

"I like her, too." That came from Alex. She was a lot like me, where she didn't let people in easily. It wasn't that she was mean, cold, shut down or anything like that. Her dad was in a career that made them move all the time. Almost every two years. I think she once told us the longest she ever stayed in one place, before moving to Massachusetts, was five years. So, she learned to not let people in easily, because she'd just end up leaving them behind.

Leah perked up a little, so far the only one not to chime in with her thoughts about Sierra. "I would like to present a motion to add a new member to our oh-so-exclusive clique. Does anyone second the motion?"

"Second."

"All in favor?" We all looked around the room, grinning at each other. "AYE!"

I looked at Leah. "Exclusive clique?"

"Yup." Her eyes sparkled but she chose not to elaborate. I don't think I wanted her to elaborate.

"Well, let's get the newest member over here, and let her get a taste of what she's now a part of. Who knows, she may end up in a fetal position in the corner, sucking her thumb, rocking herself silently after spending a night with us." I pulled out my phone and texted her, giving her my address as we laughed at the mental image.

Less than five minutes later, my doorbell rang. Damn, that was fast.

I opened the door to a much less Bimbo Barbie looking Sierra. She had a long sleeve t-shirt, yoga pants, and a messy ponytail. Except her messy ponytail looked super cute. When I attempted the messy ponytail it looked, well, messy. All the more reason for me to befriend her.

She looked at me shyly. How could someone who can ride a pole, flip around it wearing almost nothing one minute turn up here fully clothed looking nervous the next? There was definitely a story here.

"Hey, Sierra, c'mon in. How on earth did you get here so fast?" I grabbed her by the arm and pulled her in. The little orange kitten, Rescue, hopped off of Alex lap and bounded over to Sierra. I heard a totally girly squeal as she picked the little kitten up, baby talking to it and rubbing her face in Ressie's soft fur.

"I live one street over. Can you believe it?" Wow, no, I couldn't. This was proof that I'd been way too wrapped up in my little world. I didn't even know the names of the neighbors who lived on either side of me, and I'd lived here for four years.

"Awesome, we are neighbors, then. You like red wine? And chocolate? Please tell me you like chocolate, otherwise we cannot be friends."

She looked at me in shock. "If there are people out there who don't like chocolate, they obviously cannot be trusted."

"Agreed, we don't need that type of negativity in our lives." We laughed and I brought her into the living room, and pushed a glass of red wine into her right hand.

She looked down at the kitten in one arm, glass of wine in the other hand and pronounced that this was the life.

We all agreed and after only a few seconds of those awkward 'someone new is here and doesn't know all of our stuff' moments, conversation flowed easily between us. Something told me that the pole dancing thing may have been one of the best things we ever did as a group.

Chapter 12

I woke up Sunday morning with a smile on my face. I couldn't figure out why I was laughing on the inside. Until I looked at my alarm clock and realized it was Sunday. Hmmm... Sunday. Why did I feel like I had something going on Sunday that I should know about? I sat up in shock. Holy crap! The date. We'd had so much fun with our pole dancing experience, that we'd almost forgot about tonight and the blind date we had set up with Leah and Mark. I shot out a quick text to Mark:

"You still in?"

I waited, as nervous as if it were my first date as opposed to a secret group blind date for my Leah.

"Bring it."

I laughed. Bring it? What, was he a thirteen year old girl hooked on competitive cheerleading movies?

A quick text was sent out to the girls:

"You bitches better not stand me up tonight!"

I wished I could tell Leah to dress up and do make up a little more than was normal for her. But I if I did that, it would be like waiving a red flag in front of the proverbial bull. She'd have every clue she needed to figure out she was being set up. How could I give her an idea that this was dress up worthy. A lightbulb moment. You know, in the old school cartoons when Bugs would get a brilliant idea and a lightbulb would appear over his head? Yeah – I had one of those moments.

I pulled a sexy outfit out of the closet and took a picture of it. Quickly shipped that pic out to all the ladies with this message:

"Thinking of this for tonight. What do you think? Too much? Or just the right amount of sexy? May meet my future ex-husband tonight!"

I sat back and waited. I was bound to hear from someone soon. Alex first, *"Evil bitch."*

Leah next, *"Oh my gawd, I loved that outfit when we went shopping. Make sure you straighten your hair, wear some sexy ass heels and for the love of God and all that's holy, please put on make-up. And shave your legs. And, no, it is not a waste of time."*

I had to shake my head at that last bit of advice.

Karyn sent me a message privately, *"Mission accomplished."*

My phone rang a few minutes later. I looked at the display and saw Leah's smiling face.

"Hey, girlie, what's up?"

"So, I didn't know we were going to get dressed up tonight, I thought it was just dinner." Leah was always the one to pick up on changes in behavior, strange nuances, etc. She learned it after that jerk burned her. As a result, she's hyper sensitive to all changes.

"It's a really cool restaurant, one of those great places you go to see and be seen. We've never had anything like it in the area before. It's the type of place we would go to Boston or Providence for, normally. I had a blast there with Mark last week, so I wanted to share with my harem."

"Harem, nice." Leah chuckled. "Hey, you never did tell me how the date went. Or non-date. How was it?"

Oh man, here was my big opportunity. I needed to make her feel squishy over the mere concept of him, without seeming like I was into him myself.

"We really had a great time. He's very sweet. You would have loved his way of breaking the ice. Caught me off guard but we laughed so hard and it made the evening really easy. He knew how hard it was going to be for me, you know, because of Craig and all. So he worked overtime to ensure we had a great time."

"Okay, so what was the crazy ice breaker?"

"Um, how I lost my virginity."

I heard a muffled sound, a splashing sound and then coughing. A lot of coughing. And then the laughter.

"Oh my gawd, you should have warned me. I had just taken a sip of my coffee. UGH, now I have to clean that mess up. He actually asked you that? For real?"

"Yeah, after I asked where he was from. He basically accused me of having the lamest opener that ever existed. He shamed me."

"Rightfully so. I think we should have gotten together and written down possible topics of conversation for you. So, you didn't answer him, did you? You didn't tell him about... well... you know..."

"The nubbin? Yep. Told him everything." 'The Nubbin' is our nickname for the poor, unfortunately endowed man who was unable to take my virtue. Think of when you see a dog like a boxer or a cocker spaniel whose tail has been docked. When they meet you, their little stub of a tail wiggles. It's just a nubbin, not a tail. Kind of like that guy's junk. "Hey, he accused me of lameness, I had to make sure he knew I was truly epic."

"So are you guys going out again? Are you dating?"

"No, we're not. He asked me about Craig, and whether I was still wanting to be with him. I took a moment and thought about it, because truthfully, I could see myself falling for Mark. However, every image of me and someone else in my mind becomes me and Craig. It's him I want to be with, and anyone who I try to date right now is just going to be used to put a Band-Aid on my heart. It would be a rebound and that wouldn't be fair. Mark was cool, basically told me that was good. He would have been interested in dating me, but he's not into poaching. Said because I was cool and funny he'd be perfectly fine with us being friends instead of not knowing me at all."

"Wow. They still make guys like that?" Leah looked astonished.

"Yeah, they do. Not many, there's still a bunch of assholes out there, but there are a few. Mark is definitely one of the good guys!"

"Huh."

"So anyway, loved this place we went to, it has a crazy cool vibe. I know you'll love it. It's definitely a place where you would want to dress up so you can feel like the other half!"

Leah laughed. "Okay, I think I have a 'sex-bomb' outfit here somewhere, I'll send you a picture."

A few minutes later my jaw dropped. Leah had sent me a picture of herself in a dress that had a front panel in bright red, with the two side panels in black. The shape of the black panels mimicked the perfect hour glass figure. A pair of black high heel boots completed the picture. Dayum!

Another text comes over. "Is this okay?"

I shot her back a quick reply, "Hell yeah, I'd do you."

Grinning, I put the phone down and congratulated myself on setting the bait. I sent the girls the picture of Leah all dressed up. I couldn't wait to see Mark's face when he saw her in that dress tonight.

**

We decided to catch a cab to the restaurant. It's easier than having someone pull straws to be the designated driver; and then have that person sulk a little through dinner. When we stepped out of the cab it was a little 'Sex in the City'. Four women in short dresses and high heels. Yup, we looked like a bunch of women on the prowl. Thankfully we had reservations, because the wait was over an hour for walk-ins. We were seated and I quickly scanned to see if Mark was there. No sign of him, yet.

"Ash, this place is awesome. You were totally right about it." Leah was bouncing she was so excited about the place.

"Wait till you see the menu." My mouth started watering, already imagining the scallops from last week. I knew I should try something different, but I couldn't bring myself to. Maybe I'd order an appetizer to force myself to live on the edge.

"Hey, Ashley. Guess you liked it here as much as I did."

My head whipped up in surprise. I hadn't heard or seen him approach so I was really surprised to see him. That was probably a good thing because it came across as if I didn't know he was coming to the table anyway.

"Mark! Oh my gosh, it's great to see you." I took a moment to devour him with my eyes. Sometimes I hated being a loyal person. I could happily lick whipped cream off of his body. Sigh.

"Ash, you okay? Are you not feeling well?" He looked at me with concern and I realized that I had groaned a little out loud. Embarrassing. I felt my cheeks flush bright freaking red, and his eyes lit up with understanding and amusement.

"Um, yeah, I'm fine." Was still staring. Must. Stop. Staring. I heard a throat clear and looked up at Alex who gave me the wide eyed 'WTF' look as she looked at Mark. Oh, that's right, I was supposed to be introducing him to the girls.

"My manners suck, sorry about that. Mark, these are the women who have been torturing me the past several weeks in the name of blogging brilliance. Alex, Karyn and Leah. Guys, this is Mark."

As Mark shook each of my friends' hands, he made eye contact and gave them all his hot flash inducing smile. I watched their eyes light up as they got his attention. When he got to Alex, his grin turned devilish. He took her hand and said, "I do believe that you know me as Mc Hots a Lot."

She burst out laughing and invited him to sit with us. That was the ideal ice breaker for our group. Within seconds he had all three of them charmed. I could have sworn I even saw Leah looking at him with more interest than was normal between friends. She looked at me and I saw her cheeks turn pink before she turned away. Oh man, this was going better than I could have ever expected. I pictured her blushing, as we lowered a white veil over her face and led her to the aisle. I could see her walking on her dad's arm, meeting Mark at the front of the church. I must have had a pretty wistful look on my face, because I heard, "Hey, Earth to Ashley…Come in, Ash."

I shook my head and apologized for zoning.

"What on earth were you thinking about? You looked so happy." Alex lifted and eyebrow as she asked.

"Wedding." I let it out before I could stop myself.

"What?" Mark looked as if he was going to choke on his food.

"Uh, yeah, Karyn's getting married in October. Sorry, I zoned out thinking about her wedding". I looked across the table at Alex and Karyn who were both giving me the looks that called me on my bullshit. I gave back the 'what was I supposed to say' look. I loved that I could have conversations with my friends without saying a word.

Leah, fortunately, did not catch on to the eye conversation that was going on around here and chimed in, "Oh my gawd, it's going to be an incredible day. I love the dress that Karyn picked and even the bridesmaids dresses aren't nausea invoking."

At this point we all looked at Mark, who looked just plain terrified. I started laughing at the look on his face. Leave it to a guy to be freaked out about wedding talk.

There was a live band playing, and they were actually pretty good. A lot of people were starting to get up and dance. I looked at Mark and then pointedly looked at Leah to see if he would get the point that I was gently suggesting that he ask her to dance. He looked at me and his expression said "You, okay?"

Geez. Men.

"Oh, look. People are dancing! How cool that we finally have a place we can go for dinner, live music and dancing."

Four sets of eyes focused on me as if I had absolutely lost my mind. I had a feeling that I was perhaps not very good at the whole subtlety thing. I smiled weakly, while they stared at me. Finally, they returned to their conversations. I couldn't figure out how the heck to move this forward so that the two of them would find their happily ever after.

Alex looked at me and rolled her eyes. I was pretty sure she was telling me to be patient, but that had never been my greatest strength. Along with subtlety, apparently. I gave her the 'I don't know what to do' eyes. She looked at the ladies room. I opened my eyes up wide.

"I have to go to the bathroom." I jumped up as I had just realized that if I didn't go to the bathroom that very second my life would end. I gave Karyn and Alex the 'you are coming with me right now' look. Leah started to hop up, and I stopped her.

"No, Leah, you can stay here."

She started glaring at me and I knew I had to think quickly, or this was going to implode.

"Hey, I know someone that has a birthday coming up pretty soon, and she can't be a part of all group discussions." Talk about a Hail Mary! I tried not to exhale too strongly when she broke into a huge smile. As Alex, Karyn and I walked away I heard Mark ask her when her birthday was. This was the first time they'd had a chance to talk alone. I turned to watch them for a few moments, I saw her leaning in towards him as he talked to her. I saw that Alex and Karyn were watching them, too. We smiled at each other and went on our fake trip to the bathroom.

When the three of us touched up our make-up and fluffed our hair for as long as possible without being too obvious, we went back to our table. When we walked up we realized that no one was there. No Mark, no Leah. We looked at each other, very confused. Until I saw Karyn grinning from ear to ear and pointing at the dance floor. We squealed like a bunch of school girls, going into a group hug and jumping up and down.

"Oh my God, they are going to dance, and then date, and then fall in love and then make thousands of gorgeous babies."

"Whoa…slow down, Ash. How about we let them go on a first date without us first. Then we can worry about planning the wedding and future children?"

"Buzz kill." I tossed them a little side eye before we all burst into laughter. We sat down, ordered some red wine, and toasted to the hopefully budding romance between our friend and my hot teacher.

The band switched to a slow song and I could see my friend stiffen out on the floor. Mark, being the sweet guy that he is, stood a respectable distance away and bowed. He bowed like a prince in a

Disney movie, and held out his hand. I could see the hesitation in her. We all held hands at the table, held our breath and leaned forward as we waited to see what she would do. Would she dance with him? Would she turn and walk away?

She smiled. She smiled and reached for his hand. He pulled her so gently towards him, and barely laid his hand on her back. As they turned, he was facing us and looked up at our table. We all gave him a standing ovation. He was trying not to laugh at the craziness that was being one of our friends. As they slowly turned, we got in Leah's line of sight and sat down, acting like there was nothing special going on that she was dancing with a guy. This was an epic night.

When the song came to an end, Mark leaned forward and kissed her on her cheek. I could see her blushing from across the restaurant. Yup, Mark was the right choice for Leah.

We all high fived each other quickly before they returned to the table. Leah couldn't make eye contact with any of us. I announced that I was really tired and needed to go home, because I had a long day at work the next day. Alex and Karyn also said it was time for them to leave. Leah looked so upset that we were ready to call it a night, because we all shared a cab. She turned to say goodnight to Mark, and he stepped up.

"Hey, I'm not really tired yet. Leah, how about I drive you home tonight so we can stay and enjoy the band a little longer?"

I saw a battle play out on her face as she tried to decide whether he was safe. Finally, she smiled and nodded. This had gone better than I'd ever thought it would.

Even though every muscle in my body felt like it had been beaten with a lead pipe, I can't remember the last time I'd smiled this much. The pole dancing torture was almost worth it.

Almost.

Chapter 13

The decision to put videos in my last two blog posts had certainly killed any level of anonymity that I could have expected in this class. I had planned on arriving early and going to the back of the class so I would be somehow unnoticed. The thought of a dark hoodie pulled over my head and a pair of sunglasses was considered, but then rejected. That would make me look like a serial killer. So I would just sneak in, go unnoticed for the whole class. That was my plan. Well, I've heard them say that if you want to make God laugh, tell Him your plans, right? Instead of being the first to class, I was dead last. Even managed to show up after Mark. I rushed into the class room and was shocked to find only one seat left. Front and freaking center. I sat down in my seat and opened my notebook. I realized that it was very quiet in the classroom. As I looked up I saw a glint in Mark's eye and thought uh-oh. And then it happened. Dollar bills fluttered down on me from every direction in the classroom.

I looked up and around, in shock, as every classmate had made it 'rain'. Then I burst into laughter. I guess they'd read my post about the pole dancing class. I could have sat there embarrassed as I realized that everyone had seen my epic pole fail. But instead, I walked around picking up my dollars like a boss, adding a little hip swagger in, and then tucked my dollars into my tank top front. I quickly took out my phone and took a selfie with the dollars and a few classmates photo bombing. That was going up on the blog later.

Mark cleared his throat from the front of the class, getting all the attention from my dollar bill filled cleavage and back to the front where it probably belonged. He made eye contact with me, and his eyes were filled with sparkle from the smile that was fighting to not show up on his lips. I shook the girls a little, making the dollars rustle a bit. He laughed at that, shook his head and got class started.

"We only have two more weeks with each other." Some people cheered, others booed. I was surprised that the time had flown by so quickly. I really had been having fun doing this blog. I mean, some of the stuff had been just plain crazy, but it had made life interesting. So, mission accomplished.

"This week will be your last 'mandatory' blog post. Obviously, I hope you guys keep on blogging, but as far as the class is concerned, your swan song is this next post. Make it count. Next week, judgment week. You will all be given evaluation forms with the names of the blogs. You will be polite in your critique of your peer's blogging skills. After that, everyone will unveil which post was theirs. Well, everyone except for those people who thought it would be a great idea to add video, thus removing the anonymity of the blog." Everyone laughed and clapped. I stood up, doing a little princess wave to the class. "I usually bring some sort of food type refreshments on the last day. If you want to bring something, please feel free. I am not allowed to bring any type of liquid refreshment besides water, punch or soda." Groans of disappointment went around the room. Mark held up one hand, stopping us. "I said that I was unable to bring any type of liquid refreshment that was worthwhile. I am employed here. However, you all are not employed here. That is all I will say." More cheers. I won't lie… I joined in.

The rest of the class, I didn't really pay attention. I was sort of sad. I realized that I'd had more fun in the past four weeks than I'd had in as long as I could remember. Craig was right. I'd been in a rut. As much as I'd had a blast without him, it would have been really nice to come home at the end of the day and tell him about the fun stuff I'd done as opposed to typing it into my laptop, sharing it with people I didn't know and may never see.

Suddenly I realized that I had one more 'adventure'. I looked at my phone but didn't see an email from any of the girls. Strange. Maybe they'd forgotten what day it was. I shook my head and returned to the class that was existing around me. Maybe it was time to get stuck in my head less and spend a little more time in the present.

***

When I got home I was greeted with four hungry felines. I swear, you'd think I starved them with the noise they were making. I popped open a few cans of kitten wet food and a can of adult cat food for Penny. As I was getting ready to go upstairs I saw a manila envelope with my name on it on the kitchen table. I shook my head, grabbed the envelope and head upstairs to change.

I curled up on my couch with a purring pile of felines. I took a very deep breath and opened the envelope.

A photo of a beautiful home with a wraparound porch slid out of the envelope, along with a handwritten note.

"For as long as we've known you, you've talked about summers on the Cape with your family at your grandparent's house in Cataumet. However, lately you talk about the Cape as if it is this infested with locusts that have fallen from the skies. You have, in the past four weeks got some kittens, got a dangerous makeover, went on a date and sort of worked a pole. You've eaten out even though you used to loathe spending money for a meal you feel you can make yourself. The one thing you haven't done that Craig mentioned was taking a vacation. So we have booked you an overnight at a bed and breakfast on the Cape. At the beginning of the summer. Enjoy!"

I gasped and held my hand to my heart. Summer, at the Cape. Every childhood memory came flooding back to me. I loved going to the little cottage that we spend every summer at. But then my inner adult kicked the shit out of my inner child and I realized that a weekend at the Cape in the beginning of the summer meant I would be on the road with tourists. A freaking lot of freaking tourists. I groaned as the letter slipped from my fingers. Traffic. Summer people traffic. They were the bane of the existence of every resident along 495 or 25. I suddenly realized that through the years when I thought my parents were as excited to go to the Cape as I was, they were suffering through the tourists trying to maneuver our 'quaint' roads.

Grrrr. Okay. A weekend in Cataumet. I could do this. A small smile started to grow on my face. Maybe it would be fun. I could pick wild blueberries, flatten pennies on the train track, go to the old beach and just chill and read. Yeah, maybe this would be just what the doctor ordered.

Four days later, I was feeling much less charitable towards my friends.

Spend a night at a B&B on the Cape, on the weekend, in the summer. I gripped the steering wheel as if it was any one of their necks. This was why I didn't go to the Cape when Craig suggested a nice, romantic weekend away a couple years ago. Everyone in Southeastern Massachusetts knows you do NOT go anywhere near the Bourne or Sagamore bridges on weekends between Memorial Day and Labor Day. Unless you were a masochist. Damn tourists. Tens of thousands of people funneling onto a two lane road to go over some crazy narrow bridges built in the 1930s (long before the ridiculously oversized SUV's that people have become so attached to) made for hours sitting in traffic. It used to be that the locals could get by using the 'quaint' back roads that no one knew about, but thanks to GPS, even that was taken away from us. At least we had the rotaries.

I grinned with malicious glee as I thought of our rotaries or 'traffic circles' as they were called elsewhere. I think in England they call them roundabouts. They were the joy of all locals and the nemesis to all tourists. Seriously, people could not mentally handle two lanes of traffic going 50 miles per hour (speed limit is 30, I think, as if anyone ever actually pays attention to such things). The best part is, that drivers in Massachusetts – Massholes, as we affectionately referred to ourselves – commonly omit things while driving like using our turn signals. It was considered a sign of weakness letting the enemy (the other drivers) know what your intentions were and where you were planning to go. So it was not uncommon for someone on the inside lane of traffic to use the span of thirty feet to zoom across two lanes of traffic to one of four exits…without a signal. This causes break lights, potential accidents, cussing and a lot of single finger salutes. I remembered a co-worker telling me that he and a friend went to the Cape one year, and the friend panicked so much on the rotary that the ended up in the middle. Oh my God, we laughed so hard about that. Seriously, the thought of a car perched amongst the landscaped words 'Cape Cod', greeting the oncoming tourists was epic. Yes, mocking tourists was a seasonal pastime around here.

Finally Route 25 curved to the left and I could see the Bourne Bridge right in front of me, framed with bright blue, cloudless skies. Any anxiety that I held in my chest released immediately as I saw the familiar structure. I started grinning and even found myself humming along to the radio, as I transported back to when I was a young kid, in the back of the station wagon. "Ashley," my father said, pointing at the bridge, "Don't the lights look like big toothbrushes? And don't the big cement columns look like toothpaste? When I was little, that's what I saw in them." Dad always helped me look for the fun in the world. So he and I sang out "Toothbrush. Toothpaste" as we passed each of the structures. I caught myself doing it today, laughing at the silliness of it all. When I got to the middle of the bridge I quickly craned my neck left and right. On a nice clear day at the top of the bridge you can see the

Sagamore Bridge and the Railroad Bridge. Today did not disappoint. How had I forgotten how much it meant to me to go to the Cape every summer with my parents and grandparents? It wasn't a burden then (well, not for me...I wasn't driving.). I started to look forward to this weekend instead of dreading it.

I wondered if that little beach was still accessible, if so, I'd have to go there. It wasn't the nicest beach, like Old Silver Beach in Falmouth, but it was not as well-known so it usually wasn't crowded. I also had to go and put some pennies on the train tracks. Mom and I had just unearthed my old collection of sea glass and flattened pennies that I collected year after year in the ill-fated attempt at cleaning the attic. I think it was time to add to that container.

I finally got to the rotary circle and my life improved significantly. Second exit off of the rotary and I was off the proverbial beaten path. The local's version of Zen; finding an area on the Cape that tourists didn't know about. I smiled as I wove around old, narrow streets. The homes all looked like pieces of my childhood coming back together to form a photo album of memories that I'd forgotten. I almost wished someone was driving so I could sit in the back seat and soak up the scenery.

The GPS indicated that I should take a left onto Schooner Road and had me pull into the driveway of the beautiful home from the envelope.   Squeteague Shores Bed and Breakfast. Named after that little beach I remembered from my childhood. I got out of the car and slowly turned around, taking in the home, the grounds, and then the street I was standing on. I stopped and gasped when I saw what was diagonally across the street.

Tears filled my eyes as I found myself staring at a piece of my childhood. My heart crumbled as I stared at a small, one story home. It was white with these crazy turquoise shutters. I could see myself running around the front yard to the side, to the well-worn path that would bring me to the back yard. In that back yard was a bi-level patio of brick. I pictured the family gatherings that occurred there. Grandparents, parents, siblings, aunts, uncles and cousins; all of us enjoying a cookout and each other's company. I could almost taste the homemade blueberry pancakes mom would make after I picked wild blueberries out back. All the sounds, the smells and the sights of my childhood hit me at once. I reached up to wipe away a tear.

Until that moment I didn't realize how lucky I'd been to be surrounded by so much love in my early years.

"Hey, sweetie."

I whipped around in shock to see my parents standing behind me.

"How did you guys get here?"

"Oh, a little birdie told us that you were being forced into a trip down memory lane. She then told us we were required to be here." My dad frowned a little. "Alex can be a little scary sometimes, honey, did you know that?"

I laughed, sniffed, and laughed a little bit more. "Yeah, I'm aware."

We turned and walked up to the house to check in for the night.

"Um, Mom and Dad, do you remember where that restaurant is with the caboose we used to eat at all the time?"

Mom smiled at dad and then looked at me. "We already made the reservations."

Sweet. That's one of the things I loved about my parents. They knew me. "I wonder if that little gift store is still attached."

We walked inside the bed and breakfast, and got the grand tour from the owner, Mae. The home was built in the early 1900's; and my mom blissed out as we walked around. Mom has a thing for old homes. The more original the fixtures, the better. I swear, she almost had an orgasm looking at the original wide plank pine floor boards. The wallpaper was peeling in some areas, but mom and I agreed, it was perfect as it was. She leaned over to me and whispered, "I'd always wanted to get to see what the inside of this place looked like."

We walked back outside to view the gardens. As I stepped out of the house I was met with the smell of salty air. A deep inhale and I felt any stress and anxiety leaving me. Looking around the gardens, I recognized some of the plants I saw. Rose hips, bittersweet, concord grapes. Oh my gosh, the air smelled so beautiful with the smell of grapes. Over an arbor in the corner they had lilac vines growing. My mom was done at that moment, she'd always loved lilacs.

"So I hear you used to spend a lot of time down here. Where did you stay?"

"My grandparents owned the house with the turquoise shutters."

Her face lit up with recognition. "Oh my, I must have known your grandparents then. The current owner is a good friend of mine. Such a sweet lady. I bet she would love to have you over. Hold on, let me go give her a call."

With that, our hostess scurried back inside her home and we were left looking at each other in shock. Of course we would love to go in there, but it was one of those weird moments where you're not entirely sure you'll want to see the house arranged as the new owner has it, as it wouldn't mesh well with your current memories. She came back out with a huge smile on her face.

"Yup, I knew it, she's all excited to meet you. Why don't you guys head on over there before you go out for dinner tonight?" Mrs. Taylor had a glint of excitement in her eye. We thanked her and walked across the street. It felt strange knocking on the door of the home. I mean, I could still walk through the house in my mind and know where everything was. Yet I was knocking on the door like a stranger. A wonderfully eclectic looking woman answered the door with the most welcoming smile on her face.

"Come in, come in. My name is Eloise and I'm just beyond excited to have you here! Mae tells me you spent your summers in this very cottage. I cannot wait to hear what it looked like."

We walked in and looked around. My first reaction was how much smaller it looked from when I remembered. Then I smiled. Even though the furnishings were much different, it still looked like the old cottage. The smell of old fires that had been lit in the fireplace lingered in the air, giving it the rustic feeling you would expect from a cottage. The kitchen hadn't changed in the last two decades, which gave me a huge sense of comfort. We walked around, each of us pointing out a memory we had, which delighted Eloise to no end. We walked outside and I ran up the stairs to see the blueberries. They were a little overgrown, but still there. I won't lie, I picked a few, popping them in my mouth, smiling at the flavor of fresh picked, wild blueberries. Nothing like it in the world.

I turned back and approached the group. "Does the train still come by?"

"Does it ever. Twice a day like clockwork. 11:30am and 3:30pm. Let me guess, you'd like to put some pennies on the tracks." The look on my face must have been hysterical, because she let out a wonderful, melodious laugh that brightened the patio. "It's the first thing my grandkids do when they come to visit. I can't imagine it having been any different when you were a kid."

I think that maybe I loved this woman. I know I said I wanted to be like pole dancing grandma when I grew up, but if we could cross her with Eloise that would be my ideal older self. I indulged in a brief fantasy of sitting out on this patio with short, spiked silver hair, and a full, knee length patterned skirt paired with a bold colored tank top. Barefoot, of course, with hot pink painted nails. Yup, I think I had a bit of a girl crush on Eloise.

"Yeah, that was always one of the most fun things. We would try to place the pennies and coins in a pattern to get something extra cool out of them. One year the next door neighbor had a penny that split down the middle…the long way. It was so neat to see what a penny looked like on the inside!" I think I probably spoke with too much enthusiasm for someone my age. But being back here, man, it just brought back the innocent joy of childhood where pancakes made from wild blueberries you picked in your backyard were the best things ever. A time when you could walk down the tracks until you reached the downtown of Falmouth and no one worried about a bunch of kids' safety. I never really thought about it much, but damn, I missed those days.

"My mom was forcing me to clean out the attic recently, and we found a box with flattened pennies and sea glass. That was from when I was either eleven or twelve. I remember we'd tried to sell the flattened pennies to tourists." I grinned, jingling my pocket where a roll of pennies had been emptied out. "I'm ready to add to my collection."

We sat out there, drinking iced tea and talking about the area, how it has changed, what's stayed the same. It was one of the most peaceful afternoons I'd had in years.

We exchanged email addresses and phone numbers, and promised to keep in touch. She was so awesome, she offered to let us stay at the cottage instead of at the Bed and Breakfast this weekend. I looked at my dad, I was a little hopeful that we could. But I realized this was hard on him, too. You see, it wasn't just my childhood tied up in this cottage. He and his siblings played in the patio. They picked wild blueberries and laid coins on the track. They vacationed with their parents, who have been gone ten years now.

There were memories and ghosts in that cottage for him, and he wasn't ready to lay down with them.

I smiled and thanked her. We exchanged hugs and walked back to the Bed and Breakfast. As we walked back, I heard my Dad clear his throat. When I looked at him, he turned his head and wiped his face. He was so close to his parents. We all were. I felt like a selfish bitch, I didn't think about how he might feel going in there.

"I'm so sorry, Daddy." I gave him a side hug. He returned it fully, turning me to face him.

"No, don't you dare apologize. I'm a little sad, yeah, I mean, I grew up there every summer. The strange thing is that it was like the cottage but different. I expected them to walk in from their bedroom at any time. I could smell mom's perfume in there. I could smell dad's pipes. As much as it is making miss them horribly now, it let me feel like I was visiting with them. I felt like they were there, and I felt like I was at home. So thank you."

We hugged. Standing there in the middle of a little, quaint Cape Cod road, we hugged and remembered those awesome people we missed so much.

"Dinner time, 'rents. Let's go to the caboose."

Smiles sent all around. Yeah, no shock what I was doing. Changing the subject when something was getting too heavy. We made our way back to Mom and Dad's car, and I climbed in the back. Nothing like riding in the back seat to bring you back a couple decades. Dad popped in his Neil Diamond CD, and grinned at me in the rear view mirror. He knew how to get me smiling. The two of us started belting out Neil Diamond's 'Song Sung Blue' and time rolled backwards. The past few weeks have been meant to help me try to figure out who I was when no one was looking. These little 'adventures' had successfully challenged me to push past my comfort level. Right there in that moment, singing some off-key Neil Diamond with the people who brought me into existence I had found what I had been missing. I was so focused on my job, and trying to get ahead in life that somewhere along the way I forgot to just relax and live my life.

I'd gotten so used to staying up late, drinking red wine with the girls, cuddling kittens and typing up my blog posts; that I forgot what it was like to be done with the evening early. Like, 7pm early. Mom and Dad had gone up to bed when we got home. I was alone. I grabbed a blanket and went outside to sit and read on the porch swing.

I tried to read, figuring, what better time and place to get caught up on a good book than in this moment. But my mind refused to cooperate. All I could think about, despite trying my damnedest to push the thoughts away, was that I wished I was sitting on this swing with Craig. All the awesome moments I had today, and the incredible memories I was able to share with my parents, and what I really wanted was to share them with Craig. I made a decision. I would bring Craig back to this place. I would share this part of me with him, this part I had held back. I would finally, finally let him in.

***

The next morning I woke up, feeling more refreshed than I'd felt in weeks. I didn't really remember coming up to the gorgeous four poster bed in the room at the Bed and Breakfast, nor did I remember cracking open the window before I went to bed. I stretched, taking a deep breath of the sweet, salty air that made up Cape Cod.

I walked downstairs, but the entire home seemed to be empty. Perhaps I'd overslept? I look at the antique clock in the kitchen and saw that it was ten o'clock in the morning. Ten o'clock? What the heck? I couldn't remember the last time I'd slept this late. I grabbed a cup of coffee and a muffin from the kitchen and walked back out to the porch swing. I must have dozed off again because I could have sworn I heard my friends' voices. But they were twenty miles away in Wareham. Weren't they?

Suddenly the swing jerked forward and I woke up with a start, and looked up to see three pairs of eyes looking down.

"Surprise!"

"What the hell are you guys doing here?"

"We have heard about how awesome it was down here for years, so we couldn't let you have all of the fun."

"What's the best beach in the area?"

"Oh man, that's hard. I always loved Old Silver Beach in Falmouth. White sands, starfish, it's absolutely beautiful. But it's always a tourist trap." I curled my lips at the mere thought of the tourists. I totally understood that tourists were necessary for the economy, etc. But my Lord they made the lives of the locals into a living hell. I was at a hardware store last year discussing wall paint with a clerk. A woman came up, dressed to the nines, and stood between the clerk and me to ask for help from the clerk. Stepped right in front of me as if I didn't exist. As if I was beneath her. That's how those summer people treated the locals.

"Old Silver Beach it is. Get your bathing suit on, we're about to have some tanning time. Or burning time for those of us with red hair." Karyn grinned at me.

I flipped her off. Yeah, I was the only one with red hair. I ran upstairs and picked out my one piece and a cover-up. Okay, so we were going to go to the beach. I could handle this. I also grabbed my Kindle, just in case it got boring.

Running downstairs, I saw that Mae had already packed a lunch for us.

She waved off my attempts to thank her.

"I was young once, too, and there was nothing I wouldn't give to be able to back to those days with my friends and enjoy the day on the beach with them. So ladies, please, enjoy yourselves. Use sunblock, relax and I'll see you at dinner."

We hugged her goodbye as we headed out to the car. We cheered as the car kicked up gravel. Time to go cook on the beach. I had to admit, I was getting excited. I hadn't been on that beach since I was fourteen.

It took us over a half hour to find a parking place, but once we were out there, the girls were psyched to see how gorgeous the beach was. We found a spot near a volleyball net where a group of college boys were playing a game. Damn, I loved the scenery. The girls and I looked at each other and grinned.

"Nom nom nom." I made an exaggerated move of wiping the non-existent drool from my lips looking at the young boys with their chiseled chests and the glorious muscles creating a V that dipped down underneath their swim trunks. The four of us laughed, as we found we all were tilting our heads to try to see below those swim trunks. We should be arrested for looking at those boys.

Sunglasses were slid back up in place as we leaned back and enjoyed the companionship, the sound of the waves crashing, and the occasional sneak peak at the eye candy. For as crazy as my friends and I were, sometimes we were fine with just being quiet with each other.

While we were being quiet, I thought about the fact that I didn't seem to like to travel anymore. Why was that? What changed in me? Why was I so set in my routine that I was unwilling to move outside of it? Although, truth be told, after the past few weeks I'd broken out of my 'rut'. I grumbled a lot. I complained a real lot. But at the end of the day, I loved it all. Even face planting in the shoe store. I enjoyed it all.

So travel. Maybe I actually could enjoy traveling again. I thought about it. Where would I like to go? Where would be a place that I figure the amount of money I would have to spend to travel there and be a traveler there would be worthwhile?

Oh, I knew in a heartbeat. I thought of childhood dreams. I thought of eight grade Latin classes and a love of ancient civilization. Rome. I had to go to Rome. I grinned to myself. Yeah. It was time to start making my personal dreams come true. If I had someone to go with, that would be great, but it wouldn't be a requirement.

Laughing I stood up, and quietly started emptying our cooler. I ran out to the ocean and filled it with the cool water of the Atlantic Ocean. Quietly tiptoeing back, I stood so that I was between the three of them. In a quick move I poured the icy water on all three of them, laughing at their shrieks as I threw the cooler away and started running.

I couldn't hear what they were saying, but I'm pretty sure I heard the word 'war'.

As I was running, I managed to run smack into a brick wall. Or, at least that's what it felt like. When my back hit the sand I hissed, it was unreal how hot white sand could get. I looked, shading my eyes and almost wet myself. I was pretty darned certain that the vision that was before me, reaching out his hand, had posed for Michelangelo and boasted the name of David. It was a hallelujah moment where I swear the angels were singing in the background. Opening my eyes I saw turquoise eyes, blond hair and muscles. Oh, so many muscles. My lady parts started singing the Hallelujah Chorus along with the angels. My lady parts seemed to have a mind of their own these days, and apparently they could sing in harmony. It turned out that I had run into the frat boy volleyball game. Mental happy dance.

My brick wall winked at me, and started to help me up. I won't lie, I did the damsel in distress thing. Limp hand raised up to my knight in shining speedo. I was expecting sweeping kiss, one that transported me to another place and time. I was expecting an invitation to dinner, a wine and dine experience, that might possibly (would most definitely) end up in naked wrestling in the bedroom. I should be exhibiting some level of shame. I couldn't even begin to issue a summons for that shame right now. But then, my handsome 'David' looked up, his face went pale, and instead of whispering 'mi amore' he shouted "holy shit!" Okay, that did not fit into my fantasy. I tipped my head back, opened one eye and was treated to an upside down, monocle vision of my friends charging towards me. I was screwed.

I felt myself pulled away from my handsome frat boy, my arms being pulled towards the water. Damn, those women were strong. Opening my eyes I saw Prince Charming waving goodbye to me somewhat sheepishly. I flipped him off. Bad Prince Charming.

I looked over my shoulder and realized I was being pulled towards the ocean. Seriously? This was my payment for splashing a teensy bit of water on them? I started struggling, but their hold on me was pretty damned secure. When the hell did these women get so strong? I was starting to think they had been sneaking a lot more pole dancing classes than they had let on. I just gave up. Seriously, I went limp. Next thing I knew, I felt myself swinging. What the…? They were swinging me? I only had three friends, who was on my fourth limb? I opened my eyes, and saw my Adonis helping them out. Groaning, I closed my eyes because they just counted to three. I felt my stomach drop like it does when riding a carnival ride and then SPLASH! UGH, I couldn't breathe…I couldn't breathe! Salt water filled my nose and my mouth. I swear, I was the only New Englander who did not think that salt water was the bomb.

Coughing, I thrashed as I surfaced. I tried to take a breath but all I got was water. How far out did they throw me? I could hear the laughter coming from the shore. Wait a minute…that laughter was really close. I slowly moved my hand down and realized that I was in shallow water. Crud. I sat up, my hair dripping like a wet mop in front of my eye. I flung it back and opened my eyes to see my friends bent over with laughter, Alex was actually on the ground rolling, and sexy Prince Charming standing next to them grinning. I know I'd said it before, I was going to kill them.

I looked around, realizing that I was in approximately two feet of water. Wow, I must have looked like an idiot. I stood up, pulled my hair back and twisted it into a bun to keep it under control. No one wanted to see my hair in its natural wet state. Fortunately, my hair was long enough that I could put it in a bun without needing an elastic.

I conjured up a mental image of what it must have looked like, me being flung into the water, and then acting as if I was drowning. Gah, I hated having to admit but that would have been funny as hell. I would have taken part in that in a heartbeat if we were doing it to someone else. I started laughing as I went to the shore.

"You're lucky, I'm not going to kill you today." I then walked over to Alex, who had managed to pick herself up off the ground, and gave her a big, sloppy wet hug.

She squealed as she tried to push away, and managed to trip herself up, which caused her to fall backwards in the sand with a thud. When she stood up she had sand all over wherever I had hugged her. Which was awesome. Payback, yup…she's a bitch.

"Hey, you chicks are crazy. I'm Chad, the guys and I are down for a week, taking a break before summer session starts. We could play girls versus guys, if you are up for a match?" While he said that he was checking out Leah and Karyn's chests. They were wearing bikinis, and although they weren't the skimpiest ones on the beach, the boys wouldn't need much imagination as to size or shape. I could just see him salivating a little at the thought of what would happen when they served the ball, or jumped up to spike it. Yeah, no thanks.

"Actually, it would be much more fun for us to watch you boys play." That was Alex. She caught the ogling, too, and returned it in spades, pointedly staring at his junk. I mentioned before he was wearing a Speedo, right? Up until that moment, I thought Speedo's were disgusting. I mean, why did men feel the need to put everything on display like that. Looking down, seeing what his display was, I sent up a mental thank you, bless you and I love you to the woman who invented that scrap of material. Blessed scrap of material.

He had the decency to look a little bit chastised, but motioned for us to follow him as he walked back to his friends. I looked at the girls, shrugged my shoulders and followed. Who was I to deny myself a little more eye candy?

We headed back to where our towels were, and picked them up, moving closer to the game. Getting settled back down we were having a blast watching these guys play. Once they knew they had a somewhat captive female audience, they were showing off. One would flex after a spike, one would be certain to hit the ball a little harder than normal. We enjoyed ourselves thoroughly. It was fun to just relax and not have to worry about anything other than mentally undressing these men with our eyes. Which were covered with sunglasses. Besides, I wasn't completely convinced that they were of legal age. No matter how hot the guy, he wasn't worth getting arrested over.

After a few sets, we were bored, so we said our goodbyes. Suddenly phone numbers and names were scratched down on pieces of paper and handed to us as we were leaving. When we got to the car we decided to see who had gotten the most numbers. Childish, yes. Did I give a crap? Hell, no. I was shocked to see that I had the most numbers with four. Alex and Leah had three, Karyn only hand one. I'd have felt bad for her, except with the rock she was sporting on that finger, the guy who gave her number was obviously a bit of a jerk. Laughing, we balled up the phone numbers and deposited them in my car's trash bag. Yes, I have always kept a trash bag in my car. Neat freak, remember?

When we pulled into the driveway of the Bed and Breakfast, I noticed the time.

"Oh my God, It's almost 3:30pm!"

I ran inside the bed and breakfast, found my bag of pennies, and ran back out.

"C'mon, guys."

The three of them looked at each other with confusion, shrugged and followed me to the cottage where I'd spent my summers growing up. I didn't see Eloise's car, so I just walked around the side path to the back patio.

"Uh, Ash, are you sure we should be doing this?"

"No, I figured it would be fun to get a trespassing arrest today. Guys, this is the cottage I told you about. I met the current owner yesterday, and she's awesome. She said I could come back anytime to lay pennies."

"Lay pennies?"

"It's going to sound stupid, but one of the most fun things to do every year was lay pennies on the track and have the train flatten them. We'd stack them, try laying them down in patterns to see what would happen. I can't go home without laying pennies."

"Wow, girl. You know how to party." Oh the sarcasm from my Alex.

I grinned at her, jingled my bag of pennies, and said, "I'll even give you the pennies."

I looked at my phone when we made it down the hill to the tracks. I noticed some blue stains on the lips of my friends. I smiled, knowing they couldn't resist the wild blueberries.

It was 3:25, so we had enough time. I started laying pennies down on the tracks. My friends grabbed pennies and started laying them down looking like they were humoring me. But then, very quickly, I noticed that they were putting down penny set-ups trying to get a pattern. I saw that Karyn laid down a line of overlapping pennies. Leah was attempting a four-leaf clover pattern. Alex was laying down a small stack.

We stood back and waited on the train. I looked at my phone again, it was 3:31. I frowned, looking down the tracks in both locations. I hope Eloise had the times right, although, the tracks were so close to her house, I couldn't imagine her missing them. I didn't even hear a whistle letting me know the train was beyond view but on its way. Suddenly, I remembered a trick my dad and grandpa taught me. I went back to the tracks, got down on all fours and put my ear to the rail.

"Girl, have you lost your mind? What the hell are you doing?"

"Shhhhh, I'm trying to listen here."

"Uh, Okay, good luck with that." Out of the corner of my eye, I saw Alex making the 'crazy' motion to Leah and Karyn. I chuckled, I would get the last laugh on this, if the train ever came.

I put my ear down to the track again, and I waited. Finally, the low rumble came through the track. I jumped up, and went back with my friends.

"It's coming!" I started laughing at the incredulous looks on my friends faces when the train's horn blasted, breaking up the silence of the afternoon. Within seconds you could hear the train's wheels on the track, rhythmically chugging forward. It finally appeared, coming around the bend and we couldn't help but cheer as we watched the wheels attack our carefully laid out coins. As it chugged away, we ran back to the tracks to inspect our work. Not a single coin remained on the tracks, so we had to walk around looking for them amongst the rocks.

"Holy SHIT!" screamed Karyn, quickly throwing a coin down to the ground. "That freaking hurt." She started blowing on her index finger and thumb.

Oops. "Uh, yeah, I forgot about that. Um, the coins are really, really hot after having just been smushed flat. You may want to wait a second before picking them up." Karyn glared at me and flipped me the bird. I laughed at her. After waiting a few moments, we all started picking up our coins.

The girls who were making fun of me for such a silly way to spend the day were 'Oohing' and 'ahhhing' over their new treasures. We pocketed our flattened coins, and headed back up the hill and across the street to the bed and breakfast.

"I'm almost sorry to leave. I forgot how much I loved this place. I think I'm going to have to come back at least annually."

The girls gave me an identical smirk that could only have been interpreted as 'I told you so'.

"But I still hate Cape traffic."

"Sweetie, hating on Cape traffic and summer people is like our seasonal sport."

"Thanks for making me do this. And thanks for inviting Mom and Dad. It was a really cool way to spend the weekend."

I looked up at the beautiful home where I had spent the night, and then looked across the street at the small cottage that had filled my childhood summertime memories. I pictured a hot summer night, me with my hideous pink framed glasses with blue lenses, my braces and head gear, running around with two sparklers in my outstretched arms on that front lawn. Grinning at the memory, I returned to the bed and breakfast to pack up my stuff and return home.

Chapter 14

I was surprised on my drive home how much I was looking forward to seeing my kitties. Penny was finally starting to get a break from all of the nursing, because the babies were able to eat canned kitten food. Their little personalities were developing, as well, which was so much fun.

Pulling into my driveway, I saw Penny sitting in the window. She took one look at me, stood up, pointed her butt to the window and jumped down. Why did I have the feeling she was expressing her displeasure for my having been gone for two days?

I walked into the house, and called for my little fur balls. Three kittens came barreling around the corner and into the kitchen like it was the Furry 500, skidding and sliding once they hit the linoleum floor. Once they skidded to a stop, I couldn't help but laugh at the looks on their little kitten faces. They couldn't figure out how they'd ended up with all four paws splayed out on the floor. I walked around picking up kittens, getting baby head bumps and rusty purrs as a reward. The cold shoulder treatment that I was receiving from their mom must be something that comes with age. I was immensely grateful that these sweet babies still loved me, even though I'd 'abandoned' them.

I stopped short on my way to the living room. Abandoned. The reality of abandoned animals hit me like a ton of bricks at that moment. I had to do something. I had to do something to help with abandoned animals and the problems of the overcrowded shelters. I opened up the calendar on my phone and entered *'go to the shelter'* so I wouldn't forget. I knew I didn't particularly have a great experience the last time I was there, but I had to admit to myself that it was my own fault.

Sighing, I grabbed the can of cat treats and set about making peace with a pissed off cat. Oh, the exciting turn my life had taken. I laughed to myself, and realized that there was not a darned thing I would change. Well, maybe one thing. I started to feel down, until my one person pity party was interrupted by an alert on my phone.

"Make cookies."

Oh shit. Tomorrow was the end of blog class party, and I was going to make my famous 'mad good' cookies. I had made them for a family gathering once, and my niece called them 'mad good'. To me, the phrase 'mad good' seemed like an oxymoron. I mean, how could something be both mad and good? I shook my head. Kids.

I set out the ingredients I needed, and whipped up the batter. Easiest damn cookies in the world, but everyone loved them. I threw them together, set a batch in the oven, grabbed the treats and went to go bribe Penny. I found her hiding in her closet. I sat down next to the closet and apologized to her profusely. Then filled her in on everything I had been up to this past weekend. When the timer went off on the stove, I went downstairs. "Mrowl?" I had been followed into the kitchen. I tossed down another few treats, and set to putting in the next batch of cookies. Penny could apparently be bribed into forgiveness. A good thing to know.

After the last of the cookies had come out of the oven, I grabbed a bottle of wine, a cat, and started towards the living room. It was time to write up what was possibly my last blog. How would I go about typing up the experience on the Cape? It wasn't crazy, funny or exciting. Well, except for the Speedo clad boys and being tossed into the ocean. That was kind of funny. I grinned into the wine glass. Perhaps not every post required gads of humor and awkward situations. I walked through the weekend in my mind, the cottage and the feelings. My fingers flew across the keyboard, and before I knew it, submit had been clicked on and it was over.

Hmmmm. What would I do with myself now? I'd gotten into the habit of doing things for the blog, and writing about them. I thought about it for a while, and started smiling. Why did I need a weekly adventure made up by my friends? I started my own list:

1. Watch movies made from my favorite books and review. Maintain blog for this purpose

2. Learn to cook a new type of cuisine every month. Host monthly dinner

3. Volunteer at shelter

4. Learn to bake more than mad good cookies

5. Learn a new language

6. Watch a shit ton of chick flicks I never watched before because I was watching what Craig liked

7. Learn to be okay with who I was without needing a man to validate my existence.

The last one made me a little mad at myself. I mean, when did I become that woman who needed a man to make her feel more like an acceptable version of a woman? Hah! You know what? Even if Craig didn't come back, if we didn't become 'us' again, I think I'd be okay. I mean, at the very least I could say I would never again have the displeasure of pretending to watch a movie where someone was getting his head blown off.

***

Two minutes later it was Monday night and I was walking into the classroom for what was probably the last time. I was juggling my plates of cookies as I tried to open the door. I stumbled into the room and was shocked at what I saw.

There was music playing, people dancing, tons of food and adult libations. I grinned. As kind of sad as I was about this coming to an end, I couldn't resist the vibe coming from the group. One of the other classmates, whose name I never thought to get, grabbed my cookies, grinned at me, and gave me a loud, smacking kiss on my cheek. I felt laughter bubbling up as I watched the craziness unfold in front of me. Who had found a broom and how on Earth was I supposed to resist the conga-slash-limbo situation going on in front of me. Next thing I knew, I was grabbed by the hand and was pulled into the conga line that was weaving around the room. What the hell. When in Rome and all that. Step, step, kick. Step, step kick.

Before I knew it I felt warm hands on my sides, slowly making their way down to my hips, heading towards my ass. My oh-so-supple ass. I whipped around, glaring at a grinning Mark. What the hell?

I raised an eyebrow, pointed into his chest (causing a bit of a conga line pile-up).

"You are supposed to be with Leah, not rubbing up on me, sir." I gave him my most stern, schoolteacher 'you-are-in-so-much-trouble-mister' look. He just grinned at me.

"Judging by that goofy look on your face, you seem to find her acceptable?"

"Oh, my gosh, she is so awesome."

For the next five minutes, I heard him tell me all the positive attributes of my friend. Even though he was still somewhat rubbing on me, which was a turn-on (hey, I'm human, and he's hot), I was grinning from ear to ear. I mean, I'd figured that he was a little besotted with Leah, I didn't realized that he was completely infatuated with her. Jeez, that didn't take long. Mental high five for my awesome match-making venture.

Mark shook his head and laughed at himself. "I guess you already think she's awesome."

"Yup."

"So you didn't need me telling you."

"Nope."

"Are you laughing at me?"

"A whole lot, but only on the inside."

"Okay, I guess that's all I can ask for." I grinned at him, then gave him a sloppy, wet kiss. I jumped back into the conga line and step-kicked as if my life depended on it. This was turning out to be an awesome evening.

We finished the conga line and dug into the food and drink. And, oh, the drink. Everyone had brought not only their favorite food item, but also their favorite adult beverages. You know how they say you aren't supposed to mix your alcohol types? Well, we weren't exactly paying attention to their advice. I mean, who are 'they' anyway, what gives them the right to tell us how to live? Yup, I was feeling the buzz a little (a lot) so of course I was ready to take on 'the man'.

Mark finally stood up in front of us. Well, he leaned on the desk. We weren't the only ones who had been indulging, teacher was looking a little 'fuzzy', too.

"Whew! Maybe I should have given you guys restrictions with the alcohol. Not a single one of you lushes thought to bring water, or soda, huh? Okay, that's fine because today is easy for me. I get to sit back and do nothing as you come up and tell everyone what your blog was, why you wrote it, and what you learned from it. Most of you followed the assignment to the letter, especially in regards to anonymity." Yeah, everyone looked at me.

"So, get on up here and let's discuss."

One by one, my fellow blogonistas (just made that up) stood in front of the class explaining their blogs to each of us. It was kind of fun finally putting the faces to the posts that I'd read during the duration of the class.

Finally, I was called to the front. As I was the last one standing, I'd had all too much time to indulge in liquid courage. Oh, I neglected to tell you I hated standing up alone in front of a group? Well, now you know. That's why I would only do Karaoke with a group. I could sort of slink to the back a bit and hide. Today I didn't have the luxury of hiding behind anyone, so a little extra alcohol was used. Bad idea. Really. Bad. Idea. Booze and nerves are not a great combination. I could start to feel the sugary desserts and the drinks bubbling in my stomach. I willed myself to breathe evenly, stay calm, and get through this without herking my guts out.

Oh, God. This was scary. I stood up there, weaving a little bit while standing. I leaned against the desk and willed the words to come to my mouth. Nothing came out. Okay, that was a lie, a squeak came out. I'd posted pictures and videos of my embarrassing escapades online for the world to see, but when it came time to speak about the experience in front of people, all I could do was squeak.

"Picture us naked." That not so helpful tip came from one of the male classmates. I found myself looking straight at Mark, and couldn't help but picturing him wearing nothing more than what he came screaming into the world wearing. I licked my lips a little before I realized what I was doing. Bad, Ashley. Very bad! Do not mentally undress Leah's man. I must have been more than a little obvious about where my mind went because hoots and cat calls came from the class.

I turned beet freaking red, which was not a lovely compliment to my hair. I took a deep breath, let it out, and let 'er rip.

"Um, my name is Ashley, and I was blogging 'Singleish'."

"Can't hear you back here." Shit.

"I said, my name is Ashley, and I was blogging 'Singleish'. But I guess you guys have figured that out because there were videos and pictures as a part of my posts." Someone started humming stripper music. I glared at the offending classmate, but should have been grateful. The indignation I felt would push me through my fear of public speaking.

"Okay, so here's why I did this. The guy I thought was going to be my forever bailed on me. We had an argument because I was very engrossed in a book when I was apparently supposed to be listening to him complain about his work. That doesn't sound like a big deal, but it was not the first time that had happened. Or the second. I'm embarrassed to admit that it happened way too much, so he was absolutely in the right to be mad at me and even to walk away from me. He left saying that I had no direction. No drive. That I didn't want to do anything anymore, but sit at home and read.

One night my friends and I consumed wine, wine, wine, ice cream and wine. As a result, we decided that because of all the lovely parting words my boyfriend said, I should start purposefully doing new things. They signed me up for this class, and came up with the various 'adventures' that I took part in. One by one, they chose to put me in situations that they knew would challenge me. Things I would never do on my own. Things I would scoff at normally. I'd basically been double-dog dared, so I had to do everything they came up with. I hated it, loved it. I hated them, loved them. This has been a pretty cool, crazy experience. And as a result, I now have four cats, a slammin' wardrobe, a weekly private pole dancing lesson and a standing invite to visit my grandparents' cottage. I am now a little more open to new experiences. Oh, I'll still bitch about them. But I'll maybe do them. Maybe."

I scurried back to my seat, my eyes trained on the floor, my hands, my feet, my desk. Anything but making eye contact with anything remotely resembling a human being. I still was fighting the nausea, so the more I focused on my breathing and finally my heart rate got back to normal. I looked up to see a very concerned looking Mark asking me 'What the hell?' with his eyes. I shook my head, gave him the 'Not now' look. He shook his head at me, and turned to talk to the class.

"Okay, guys. Then, I guess that is it. You all have been awesome to work with, and I've really enjoyed getting to know you guys. I hope you will continue to take enrichment classes, and find ways to expand your horizons. Here's where I have to beg you to write nice things about me. I'm passing out a form where you have the opportunity to assess this class, how much you absolutely loved it, learned gads of information and would hate to see it ever be cancelled."

While I was waiting to get my form, I sent a quick text to Leah, asking if she would come pick me up. My reason was dual purpose. One, I'd honestly had a little bit too much to drink. I mean, I was pretty sure I could make it home without incident, but I knew it would be wrong of me to try. Second, I wouldn't hate to see Leah and Mark together again. They seriously were so freaking cute together.

When I got my form, obviously I wrote nothing but praise for Mark and glowing reviews of the class. I packed up my stuff and waited till everyone had left before walking up to Mark.

"Hey, Leah's going to come pick me up, not sure I should be driving with the varied volumes of alcohol I just consumed. Are you okay to drive? I'm sure she wouldn't mind giving you a ride." I turned another lovely shade of red, realizing the double entendre that I had just thrown out of my mouth. "I mean, um, a lift… she'd love to give you a lift." Damn.

Mark didn't even bother to try to hide his laughter. Once he came up for air, he was still smirking at me. "I might just have to take her up on that ride."

Ugh. I admit, I did a face slap. Sometimes I needed to figure out to think about what I was saying before it popped out of my mouth. "Shut up, you dope." Yeah, that was all I had. I would come up with something beautifully snarky in about thirty minutes. Twenty nine and a half minutes too late. I threw a cheesy puff at his head, laughing as it got stuck in his hair, orange powder sprinkled his forehead. I never said I was above childish food fights. If anything, I strongly encourage them.

I was laughing at how I'd 'gotten' Mark, when suddenly, something wet and a little cold hit the side of my face. I looked up with my face in a frozen 'what the hell just happened' mask. I touched my face and came across with chocolate frosting. That rat bastard threw a cupcake at my face. He ruined a perfectly good cupcake. Oh, that was an act of war. There was never a reason to ruin a cupcake. Especially not a gourmet freaking cupcake with the most amazing chocolate buttercream frosting on it. I was so going to get him back…after I finished this orgasm inducing frosting. My eyes rolled back in my head as I tasted more of that confectionary heaven.

"What the hell happened in here?"

Eek. I flinched, ducking down a little as I looked towards the door, where Leah stood, fists pushed into her hips. The look she threw our way was as if she had caught a couple of naughty school children in the middle of loading their straws with some nasty, wet spit-balls.

"Uh, sorry, Leah." I ducked my head to hide the huge smile on my face. I mean, yeah, I just got caught in a food fight with her future husband, but the fact that I had managed to bring them back together in a way that was inconspicuous was freaking awesome.

"Oh, Mark had a bit to drink, tonight, too. Are you able to drive him home tonight, too? We'll find someone else to bring us back to our cars tomorrow.

"I, uh, I mean, um…" Leah looked at me in panic. I knew why she had the fear in her eyes. How could I convince her that Mark was safe? Turns out, I didn't have to. He walked over to her, his eyes soft, gentle as he reached out and lightly touched her lower back.

"I'd really appreciate it, Leah, but I understand if you aren't comfortable with it." Mark spoke to her low, so I could barely make out the words he said.

I watched Leah's shoulders relax, her entire demeanor change. I thought I might have seen her even lean back into his touch, but I must have imagined that. You know, I drank 'too much' and all that. As we walked out of the classroom, I saw him barely brush her hand with his, and saw her reach for him just a little bit. Mark turned out the lights and locked the door. Which was great, because it plunged the hallway into a bit of darkness that allowed me to grin uncontrollably. There was just something so freaking cute about the two of them finding each other.

I chose the back seat on the ride home, claiming that my head hurt and I just wanted to lie back a little. Truth be told, I was fine. I really didn't need the ride, I was pretty sure of that. Not necessarily one hundred percent sure, but at least mostly sure. Watching two people working out the initial steps of their relationship was interesting. He wanted more, but knew he couldn't move too quickly or she would run like a skittish rabbit. She thought maybe she might want a little more but was scared that by wanting it, she would jinx it, and he would find a reason to walk away from her.

Yeah, you know what my money was on. I grinned as I settled into the back seat. I started to doze off, pretty darned please myself at the fact that I knew to bring those two together.

***

I fell asleep with a smile on my face, and woke up with the same stupid smile on my face.

It's funny how some things in life made mornings okay, and other things made you want to beat the shit out of anyone who came within five feet of you. This was a birds are chirping and sun was shining type of morning. I didn't care that I'd had a late night and had to get up extra early to go get my car from the college. Just seeing the look on Leah's face when she saw Mark made it worthwhile. I loved how I could tell she was fighting herself when it came to her attraction to him. It was going to make things interesting watching them.

A couple cups of coffee into my morning, and I was somehow pulled together to make it through the work day. I looked at my phone when a text came in. It was Leah letting me know she was downstairs waiting to 'drive Miss Daisy' to her car. Gotta love a girl who speaks in movie references.

I hop in shotgun and turn to look at her with the biggest shit-eating grin on my face.

She glared at me, looked straight ahead and focused so intensely on the road ahead of her that I was pretty sure the car in front of us was going to explode. I started picturing a Godzilla type monster, with Leah's face and laser beams shooting out of its eyes, slowly walking up and down the street blowing up cars and buildings.

I started giggling, I couldn't help myself. Obviously, she figured out that I wasn't as inebriated as I tried to let her think last night. She probably also figured out that I called her specifically because of Mark. A light blush started creeping up her neck towards her cheek. Hmmm, I wonder what exactly happened last night after they dropped me off? Oh, what the hell...

"So, was Mark okay?"

Her head whipped towards me and she had this terrified look on her face.

"What do you mean?"

"Last night? When you dropped him off? I know he'd had a little bit too much to drink. Was he okay?"

"Oh. Yeah, he's fine."

"Wait, what did you think I meant?"

"Nothing." There was that blush again. Holy mother of God, she did do something with him.

"You little tramp! Something happened, didn't it? What happened?" I was bouncing up and down in the seat like a little kid awaiting an ice cream come. Crap, now I wanted ice cream. Focus, Ash.

"Nothing happened. End of discussion. I will not say another word and you had better not ask any more questions or even think of linking my name and Mark's in a single breath to Karyn or Alex. If you do. I'm done."

Damn. She must really like him. I know it didn't seem like that, I mean, she was acting so pissy. But that's just Leah. Her best laid plans weren't quite working out like she'd, well, planned.

I just kept smiling, but didn't say a word. She groaned, and slouched down in the driver's seat. Dead silence ensued, followed by some skin searing looks.

I smiled sweetly, hopped out of the car and shouted, "Later, hooker."

She gave me the single finger salute and pealed out of the parking lot. I was doubled over in laughter. I really shouldn't be enjoying this as much as I was.

'chirp'

I looked down at my phone to see the picture of a middle finger, the caption read '*Hate. You.*' Oh man, if the Leah-Mark saga continued like this, I wasn't going to have to go to the gym for the medball workouts. My abs were sore from all of the laughing. Best workout ever.

Shaking my head, I walked to my car and headed off to work. Something told me this was going to be an incredible day.

***

'chirp!'

I should probably silence my phone when I'm at work. I looked around quickly to see if anyone had heard my phone go off. I guess the good thing about having your own office is such things can go by un-noticed. I looked down at my phone to see my reminder I set about helping out at the shelter. Crap, almost forgot about that. I looked at the clock, just about lunchtime so I could get away with doing something small that was not necessarily work related. I pulled up the website for the shelter to see what type of volunteer opportunities they might have. Cleaning, cat cuddler, event help, fundraising help. All of that seemed fairly straight forward. I had to admit, I gag enough cleaning a litter box for four, thirty or so might kill me. A pop-up came on the screen with the shelter's wish list. Bleach, paper towels, cat food, kitten food, toys, blankets, newspapers... Wow. They really needed a lot of stuff. I had to go to the pet store anyway, time to upgrade to a much bigger litter box. Those kittens were growing like crazy and one little box was no longer enough for all four. I emailed myself the list. I always did enjoy retail therapy.

After work I went to our local pet store and got a little of everything for the shelter. I also bought what could only be considered a king sized deluxe litter box. That sucker scooped itself. SCORE! I did my best not to have a minor heart attack as I saw the total. $291.67. Two hundred and ninety one dollars and sixty seven cents. I broke into a sweat as I swiped my credit card. The cats needed me, and truth be told, I could just back off on some of the wine consumption for a few months and that difference would be made up in no time at all. I stood a little taller. Tax deduction, tax deduction, tax deduction. That was my soothing mantra as I walked back to my car. I had to admit, I was a little nervous heading back to see the General. Let's face it, my last encounter with her Evil Empress did not go very well. I'm not saying she was wrong (she wasn't) but still. I was terrified of her.

When I got to the shelter, I walked to the front desk, to see if they had some sort of cart I could use to bring in all the stuff I brought. I was asked to wait a second as they brought a kennel helper out with the cart. I was really surprised when they helped me load everything up and bring it to the front. It would have taken me a few trips to bring everything, so that was really cool.

Walking back up the front desk, I waited in line for my turn. I was surprised that there was no reaction to my being in the lobby. I mean, after my last visit where I was run out of the shelter by the Director while she was practicing her broom riding, I guess I expected a wanted poster of some sorts at the front desk. I wondered if there was some sort of un-wanted poster or something that would have a horrific mug-shot style photo of me.

"Hi, may I help you?" Huh, that looked like a genuine smile. I looked at her name tag. 'Esther'. Oh man, even her name said sweet little old lady who I wanted to adopt as a grandmother so that she could come to my house and make me cookies.

I tilted my head for a second and just looked at her, willing her to recognize me as the evil spinster who was intent on starting an in-house cat colony for the criminally single.

"Ma'am?"

Ugh, ma'am. So I must look a little old when a really nice woman who is just a decade or two younger than Moses calls me ma'am.

"Uh, yeah, sorry. Spaced out there a bit. I brought some things from the wish list I found online. I'd also like to talk to someone about volunteering." I bit the corner of my lower lip. I couldn't figure out why I was nervous about this. I mean, they were all but begging for help, weren't they?

"Oh, wonderful. Thank you so much! Let me go get Sandy." I had to say, I was loving this place today. I was about to kidnap Esther and turn her into my cookie-making hostage. And now a Sandy? A Sandy had to be a nice, lady, too. It was just a nice sounding name. I stood waiting a few minutes, waiting for Sandy to come out to see me. I heard the footsteps approaching, and fixed a smile on my face, kind of excited to meet this person I felt was destined to become a new friend.

Pure ice of terror ran through my veins as she who was previously named General Kitty Litter turned the corner. I started trembling a little, and mentally located the closest exit in the event I needed to evacuate. As she continued towards me, I found myself inadvertently taking a step back. Then another one.

"Hi, I hear you're interested in volunteering, and that you brought us a bunch of donations? That is awesome, we really need all the help we can get. Do you have a few seconds to sit down and chat so we can figure out what you'd enjoy the most?" She flashed me a brilliant smile as she gestured that we were going into what appeared to be a small conference room.

"Normally, I'd have you come into my office, but it looks like a bomb went off in there. We are applying for a huge grant, so my office has been taken over by piles of paper."

I followed her numbly into the small room. I mean, I was in total shock. This woman had all but grabbed me by the scruff of my neck and tossed me out last time I was here. Now she was standing here smiling at me, joking with me and being, well, friendly with me. I must have had one hell of a facial expression because she leaned forward with an odd 'I'm a little worried about you' look on her face.

"Are you okay?"

"Um, yeah. I guess. Are you sure you don't want to throw me out?"

"Why on earth would I want to do that to you? You just brought us donations that we really, really need, and you're going to volunteer. I am so confused." She honestly looked as if she was a little upset that I would think that of her.

"You don't remember me at all, do you?"

"No, I mean, I see a lot of people, so if we've met before, I'm really sorry that I don't remember your name. But I don't know why that would mean I'd kick you and your help to the curb."

My jaw dropped. I really had expected that the interaction before had made an impression on her as much as it had for me.

"How do I know you?"

Gulp.

"About five weeks or so ago, I came in to adopt."

Her face lit up, I could tell at this point she figured she knew me because I'd adopted something from the shelter and must have met her at the time of adoption.

"So, I put on my adoption application that the reason I wanted to adopt was basically because I had been dumped, and was destined to live out my life all alone. I may have put in that I wanted an armload of cats."

I cringed, waiting for the onslaught.

I waited.

I opened up one eye and looked at her. She had her forehead in her hand and was slowly shaking her head back and forth.

She looked up at me slowly and I braced myself. I grabbed the strap of my purse to start to pull it on my shoulder so that I could leave.

"Oh man, I am so sorry I was horrible to you that day. You caught me at the worst possible time. We had just come back from a raid on a cat hoarding situation. Eighty one cats in a small house, some of them didn't make it. When I heard that you wanted an armload of cats, I snapped. I'm really not that much of a bitch, normally. And I'm sorry that I said you'd never be allowed to adopt ever again. Also sorry I called you a crazy-ass bitch that shouldn't be allowed within ten feet of a cat."

"Wait a minute, you never said that to me."

"Oh. That could have been after you left. Anyway, if you want to adopt, it's cool. You're more than welcome to adopt from us. Just, you know, maybe not an armload."

I started laughing. I mean, part of it was probably nervous laughter. But still, I couldn't believe this. So not what I expected.

"Uh, I am not exactly in the market for cats right now." I proceeded to tell her what happened after I walked out of the shelter.

She got a little bit of a hardened look in her eyes again when I explained about the kittens.

"So are you going to want to bring them in to be surrendered for adoption?"

"Now look who's bat-shit crazy! Hell, no, I'm not giving them up. They are named, happy, living out their life eating me out of house and home. They've already had some shots, are due in a week or so for the next round. I'm going to get everyone fixed. But they're going to get to live out their lives together."

She grinned at me. I figured this probably wasn't the norm. What a sad state we were in as a society when animals were so readily disposed.

We spent the next half hour talking about the kittens, about how I could help out, and a schedule was set for me to come on Tuesday nights to help clean cages and cuddle kittens.

I was right this morning. It had been a pretty incredible day.

Chapter 15

The next day when I was at work, my euphoria over Leah and Mark, kittens and volunteering disintegrated like dust. Around 1:00pm, I got an email from Alex.

"So, this Friday night is Karaoke Spotlight night at Eatz. You have to pre-register because it's a competition of some sort. A local thing, life time supply of clams or some kind of cheesy Cape Cod touristy thing. Anyhow, for your next challenge, I've signed you up. You have to be there at 7pm."

What. The. Hell.

I quickly shot back an email to my 'friend'. Yes, her status in my life was in serious question.

"You must be smoking some incredible shit to think that I would be doing anything remotely close to that. One: school's out, so no more challenges. Two: I don't do public speaking or singing. Drunk group karaoke doesn't count. So you can take your challenge, roll it up niiiiiice and tight, and shove it!"

Yeah, no way in hell. If I couldn't stand in front of a group of my 'peers' to talk about the blog I knew all of them had read, I was not going to go up and sing. Just the thought of singing alone in front of a group of people made me feel all sorts of nauseous. I had to think of something else, I was hyperventilating about this. No way. There was nothing she could do or say to make me do her stupid 'challenge'.

'chirp'

I looked at my phone where a text message had come through.

"I dare you."

Oh my God, I hate that bitch so much. The word 'dare' was my kryptonite. I could never resist one, no matter what, and she knew it. I started shaking, both from fear and pure anger.

I was going to have to sing in front of people. On Friday. In two days. Oh, man, this was beyond my wildest fears.

I wanted to type back something to express to her the level of 'oh hell no' I was feeling, but no. I didn't feel like giving her the satisfaction of knowing she'd gotten to me. She fed off of such things. It was how she got her power.

I spent the remainder of the day being asked non-stop if I was okay, if I was feeling fine, being told I looked a little pale. I'm a redhead naturally. For someone to think you look pale when you were already a shade of white only slightly darker than a piece of paper was alarming.

I stopped making eye contact with people in the hallway. If I had to say 'I'm fine, thanks' one more time, I was going to headlock someone tight enough that their well-meaning but highly annoying head popped off of their insignificant neck. I shuddered at the mental image. I wasn't normally that violent a person, and whenever I watched a movie that had violence I hid behind pillows and blankets. Maybe I should take these lemons and turn them into limoncello and start my own drinking game? Every time I heard 'Are you okay?' it's one drink. If I heard 'You don't look so good', it's two drinks. That would make my day a hell of a lot more interesting.

I walked towards the ladies room and was stopped by one of the admins, Cathy.

"Hey, Ash, are you okay? You're not looking so good."

I couldn't help it, I started laughing as I told her I was fine. Mentally I took three drinks. Meanwhile, Cathy looked at me as if I was already drunk. That had me giggling even harder.

I finally made it to the ladies room, where I splashed a little cool water on my face. When I saw myself in the mirror, I actually scared myself a little bit. Dayyyyum, no wonder everyone was worried about me. My face was almost translucent it was so pale, and there were dark, purplish half circles under my eyes. This was not acceptable.

I pinched my cheeks hard enough that a little, pitiful 'yelp' made it past my lips. I looked at my face again. I decided it was at the very least an improvement.

Once I got home, I bypassed my laptop, for fear of what I might find on it. Probably more details of my psychological undoing courtesy of my former friend, Alex. Instead, I went to my old friend, my Kindle, and a glass of red.

I flopped on the couch. I supposed I should say I reclined and make it sound much more ladylike than it was, but it was a flop. Within seconds of getting comfy cozy I heard the rumbling of my black and white princess.

"Hey, Penny, how was your day today, girlie?"

"Mrowl!"

"Mmm, really? They did that? What else?"

"Mrrrrowl!"

Yeah, I was having a conversation with my cat. And I was pretty sure she was trying to tell me something about the kittens and what they all did today while I was working. I shook my head at the absurdity of it, and took a nice, long sip of wine.

I heard little claws attacking my sofa and before I knew it, my entire furry family and I were curled up together on the couch and as I powered up my Kindle I let myself relax into the world of Scottish lairds fighting for the honor of their headstrong women.

I woke up four hours later, with a wicked crick in my neck. I looked up and saw that the kittens had positioned themselves all over the couch and I had contorted to accommodate them. Mom cat was smart and was sprawled out on the top of the couch cushion. How did such tiny beings take up so much space?

I stretched, rolled my neck and tried to maneuver myself off the couch in a way that wouldn't disturb the cats. Yeah. I know. Judging by the swatting at my legs, I was unsuccessful. I scooped up Penny and went upstairs to the real bed for the last two hours of sleep. Penny seemed a little disgruntled, but purred as she padded around in a circle, finally curling up nice and tight next to me, falling asleep instantly. I felt more than a bit jealous that she could fall asleep so quickly, while I laid there wide awake, still dreading the day after tomorrow. Her purring got louder and louder, and I found myself relaxing. It seemed as if cat purr was my relaxing spa music. As I fell back asleep, I had a small smile on my face.

***

Have you ever noticed that when you're looking forward to something happening, the time drags on and it seems like forever until 'that day' arrives? But when it something that you are dreading, by God there's just a snap of the fingers and that day is there, staring you in the face, about as welcome as a zit on your nose on the day of a huge interview.

Friday night already. At five thirty I was pacing around my house, alternating between 'screw it, I'm not doing this' and 'dammit, it was a dare and I have to do it'. Yeah, I know. I was weird about the whole 'dare' thing. But it was what it was and I found myself tossing on some jeans, sandals, a t-shirt and I was out the door.

I don't know why, but I didn't think this would be any big thing. But as I pulled onto Seashore Drive, my stomach sank when I saw that there were no spots. No parking spots at all. I drove around, finally finding a place about four blocks away. Fan-freaking-tastic. Breezy summer evening, plus the humidity of living near the ocean and my hair went *poof*. You know how the main character in Brave has ALL that hair? Well, add a bit of frizz to that you have what I looked like walking into the restaurant.

As I looked around the room, I had to swallow around what felt like a growing boulder in my throat. I felt chilled looking at the standing room only crowd, yet I realized I was sweating as if I'd run a marathon. I bee-lined for the bar, knowing that I was going to need liquid courage to get me through my fear of doing anything in front of a crowd. It was going to take a couple glasses of wine (at least) to get me loosened up enough to do what I had to do. I gulped the first one back in an embarrassingly record time. The second I held onto and did some much more ladylike sipping as I walked over to sign in. I then found a section of wall that appeared to be in desperate need of being held up and I leaned against it, willing myself to disappear.

In what seemed like no time at all, I heard a thumping noise, and then what seemed to be the obligatory feedback you get whenever someone makes an announcement from the stage.

"Hi everyone, and thank you for coming to the first annual Cape Karaoke Star contest. We have ten brave souls who are ready to stand up here and sing their hearts out for you tonight. Your applause will be taken into consideration by the judges as to who the winner is. The winner, in addition to a crazy level of bragging rights, will be getting a hundred dollar gift certificate here at Eatz, a clam bake from 'The Crazy Clam' and a gift basket of items from local vendors. The gift basket is up on the bar for anyone who wants to look. Please remember to shop local, it makes a difference and keeps businesses here in town."

He paused as the applause was a little off the charts for the local businesses. Hey, I joined in. I'd like to keep an awesome downtown area because that meant more shopping. Shopping made me happy. I liked being happy.

"So without further ado, let's get this thing started!"

The first person was called up. I didn't know her name, but I had to say I recognized her from around town. She wasn't half bad, having picked an Aerosmith song to start out the night. Smart move.

I had to give her mental props for that one. When you are from Massachusetts, you are obliged to love a few things in life. The Red Sox, the New England Patriots, cranberries and Aerosmith. Even my dad likes Aerosmith, and this is a man who enjoyed the musical styles of The Kingston Trio; Peter, Paul and Mary and Simon and Garfunkel. It's a local thing.

I looked around the room as the patrons were tossing back their beers, cheering her on, cringing when she went perhaps a bit flat or too sharp. But all in all, everyone was really nice about it all. No one heckled her. But then again – they'd just started drinking. Oh my God, what were they going to be like when they'd had more than just a half of a beer in them? For the first time since this whole thing started I wanted it to be sooner rather than later.

"Pick me, pick me, pick me…."

"Our next contestant is going to be…Aaron Hale. C'mon up, Aaron!"

Crap.

He chose a song by Guns and Roses. He honestly wasn't very good, but he was moving around the stage, hopping all over the place, adding in hip thrusts, attempting sexy moves (which weren't very sexy). Women actually threw a couple of dollar bills his way when he started to pull up his shirt to show his one pack. Yes, his one pack. It wasn't necessarily pretty, but it was funny as hell. I found that I was cracking up watching the whole thing, and started to get into the party atmosphere. I guess I didn't have to worry about whether I was any good or not. This was all just supposed to be fun.

My epiphany came to an end when I heard the next name announced.

"Ashley MacKillop, come up to the stage. You're next!"

There was polite applause. The type that you do when you know you should but you don't know whether the person you are about to see deserves it or not. I guess this was it.

I pushed myself away from the walk that I was holding up and set my glass of wine that had somehow managed to get empty on the bar. I made my way to the makeshift stage with a bit of dread filling my stomach. I started to give myself a mental pep talk.

"You can do this, Ash. You've got this. You know this song inside and out. This is no different than singing in your car, or in the shower. Except there are people here. People are watching you.

People who aren't in your shower with you because that would make you all sorts of nasty. Just sing."

I had a sneaking suspicion that my little pep talk was all sorts of useless. Oh well. At least I was able to sort out whether I was nasty or not, and I was not. I stopped by the guy who was running the music and told him my selection and got out to the microphone. I looked up and involuntarily took a step back. Over a hundred people looks a lot different when you are standing in front of them as opposed to being one of them. I felt my heart pounding, my hands got icky sweaty and my stomach bottomed out again. Oh. My. God. I could not do this. I started to turn to walk away when I heard the first note of my song. The intro to 'My Baby Loves Me' was really short, so I had to stand up there and try to deliver. It was officially too late to run.

I automatically started singing along with the song, because I just knew it that well, but there was no power. I sounded weak and airy. I knew it was fear and as I looked out I saw looks of pity from around the room. I was bombing. I closed my eyes and pictured myself in the car singing it. I realized that in my mental projection, I was riding shotgun with Craig in the driver's seat. I could feel his hand in mine, our fingers intertwined. I'd forgotten. I always sang this song to him. This song was my love note to Craig. I opened my eyes and started the next chorus with a smile, and started rocking out my inner Martina McBride.

"He never tells me I'm not good enough, just gives me unconditional love…"

I was belting it, finally. I was singing this to Craig. He wasn't there. God only knew where he was. But in my heart, I knew I was singing to him. I guess I hoped a little bit that somehow his heart would speed up wherever he was, and somehow, cosmically, he'd know.

I got to the chorus and my fear was gone. I was cat-walking the stage, shaking my hips, leaning back with the high notes. Yeah, in my head, I was all sorts of divalicious.

All of a sudden I realized, it was over. The last notes hung in the air, and there was silence. Uh-oh, did I really blow it or did I sound good.

I squeaked out a 'thank you', and suddenly, it was there. Applause. I never knew I liked the sound of applause so much. I blushed ten shades of red and scampered off of the stage. I'd love to tell you I held my head high, waved to everyone and sashayed off. But, no. I scampered. Hurried my happy ass off the stage as quick as I could without managing to stumble, fall and make a fool of myself.

I started to walk towards the entrance, to get ready to leave. I knew it was a contest and all, but I also figured there was no way I had won. I mean, I had crazy stage fright at the beginning. Besides, that wasn't what it was about. It was about the damn bet.

Suddenly, I was jerked backwards and pulled in to a squealing, jumping hug.

"You did it! I knew you could do it. I always knew you could." I finally came out of my shock enough to realize that the jumping was courtesy of Alex.

"I can*not* believe you did that to me. You are the most evil, horrific person in the entire universe to dare me to do something that you know I'm terrified of, when you know I can't walk away from a dare. Do you know how awful this was for me? Do you know how sick to my stomach I was since Wednesday? I should totally kick your ass for this."

Alex looked at me with round eyes. I'd clearly never laid into her like this. But I was mad. Still mad. Even though it went well, even though I kind of had to admit to myself that I enjoyed it. Even though she made me face my fears, pull up my big girl panties and just do it. Even though…aw, crap.

"Thank you."

She looked shocked, probably as shocked as I felt inside that I'd just thanked her. But I figured it out. She made me face my fear, and slightly overcome it. She did it to help me, not humiliate me. She threw her arms around me again and I hugged her back just as fiercely. When I opened my eyes, I stopped breathing.

Six weeks. Or was it seven now?

I saw jeans that were too damn sexy to be worn in public, but maybe I was the only one who saw them that way. I saw a brown Beatles 'Let It Be' t-shirt that showed off his muscular arms. And I saw soft brown eyes, that were looking into mine with a little bit of sadness, a little bit of regret, a little bit of fear but a lot of love.

Craig.

Craig was here. In this place.

Craig heard me sing my song, the song that was always his. He heard it all.

Tears filled up my eyes. I wanted to run and jump into his arms. I wanted to feel those arms around me, holding me tight. I wanted to kiss those lips until we were less than politely asked to 'get a room'. I wanted all of that. I just stood there. I realized my mouth was slightly open and I closed it. The tears started to spill out of my eyes and down to my cheeks.

Shit.

I didn't believe in letting people see me cry. If they saw me cry, they'd know that they'd 'gotten' me. I couldn't let that happen. I quickly wiped at my cheek and turned to run the opposite direction. The only escape I figured I could find was the ladies room. I went in and locked myself in a stall and let it out. I had my ugly cry. Where the hell had he been? Why hadn't I heard from him? What right did he have to look so damned delicious that I wanted to have him for breakfast, lunch, dinner and dessert?

I heard the door of the bathroom open and a herd of footsteps came trampling in. And of course, they stopped right in front of my stall.

"Ash, we know you're in there. C'mon out, okay?" Leah sounded so worried.

I walked out and headed for the mirrors.

Ugh. That's why they are referred to as ugly cries. My face was red and splotchy all over. My eyes were red-rimmed and bloodshot. My nose was running. I dropped my chin to my chest in defeat.

"Guys, he was here. Craig was here. Why on earth was he here, tonight of all nights?

"Uhhhhmmmm, because I kind of told him he could come." That very quiet admission came from Alex.

"What do you mean you told him he could come? I don't understand. When did you talk to him?"

"Wednesday."

"Wednesday? As in the date you told me about this god-awful stunt you had planned for me? That Wednesday?"

"Yeah. And then every Saturday before then."

I had no words. Every ounce of air whooshed out of my lungs at the enormity of her deception started to sink in. She'd known where he was. She had talked to him. She had seen my pain and did nothing to help.

"How... why... *why?*"

"It started right after he left you. After the four of us had met up and had wine, ice cream and some more wine. When I got home, I called him up and chewed him out but good for being a brain-dead asshole for breaking your heart. I called him much worse than that. He quietly listened to me letting him know how much I hated him for hurting you, and then I heard it. He sniffled a little. He was crying. As broken as you were, he was as broken. He told me he just was angry at feeling ignored and just lashed out. He didn't know how to even try to fix what he'd said, because he couldn't ever really take it back."

She took a deep breath, and gave me a look that spoke of determination, nerves and of a hope for forgiveness. I braced myself. I had a feeling that whatever it was she was about to tell me was NOT going to be good. Not at all.

"I told him what we were doing. I told him about the wine, about the ice cream, about the tears. I told you were going to do this blog with these weird challenges. I told him to stay away. I told him you needed a chance to be you without him, and that you had to figure out how to enjoy your own company as an individual. He told me he was going to go on a work trip for a couple of weeks. I thought that was a good thing for you guys to have some distance. I let him know the blog address once you started it so that he could see what was going on. He has been communicating with me to check in on you. He wanted to come to you, but I told him it wasn't time.

The reason I set up this last challenge was for you two. I figured it was about time you guys get a chance to work this couple thing out now that you've worked yourself out."

I couldn't speak. Twice now in one night I had been rendered speechless by people I trusted implicitly. Correction. People I had trusted implicitly. Very much past tense. I backed out of the bathroom, shaking my head, my cheeks were wet with tears I wasn't even aware that I had shed. Alex's tears mirrored mine. She started to take a step towards me but I held up my hand.

"No. You do not get to come to me, touch me, talk to me or try to console me. You have given up the right to have a part of me anymore. The four of you. I...I don't even know how to look at you.

You all were manipulating my life. You were playing with my feelings, my emotions. You told me to face the facts that he might not come back to me, all along you were keeping him away. I'm done."

With that, I turned and walked out the bathroom and straight to the front of the restaurant. I saw Craig stand up out of the corner of my eye, but I just shook my head at him and kept walking. When, I got outside, I took a deep breath of the cooling summer night air. I started walking towards my car at a break neck speed. I heard his footsteps behind me and started to walk faster.

"Ash, please, honey." I whipped around at that and glared at Craig.

"Honey? Honey? I'm sorry, perhaps you are speaking to someone else, because I am sure you are not calling me honey. I haven't seen you for about six weeks. I haven't heard from you in about that same amount of time. And you think you can call me honey? Oh, hell no."

I turned and started walking again, when he spoke.

"Ashley, I'm sorry."

I stopped. My shoulders slumped forward in a bit of defeat as I waited to hear what else he had to say.

"I'm so sorry that I walked away. I was so angry and felt so freaking ignored, like maybe you didn't care whether I was there or not. I'd had a shit day, and it was just the straw that broke the camel's back. I lashed out and said stuff I absolutely should not have said. I didn't want a break. I wasn't done, not with us. Never with you. The next day I found out that I was being sent out of state for a couple weeks to help ramp up the new offices in Detroit. I was freaking out about what happened between us, and when Alex called I just lost it. I was a sobbing mess, but I listened to what she said, and I thought it made sense at the time.

When I came back, it no longer made sense. I wanted to see you. I wanted to be with you, hold your hand, to hear your voice. I would have paid money to see you on the couch reading some romance novel. I read your blog. I read about all of your adventures, and I wanted nothing more than to be there with you. I wanted to meet the cats. Did you know I absolutely love cats? I am just so beyond sorry that I did this to us. Is there any way that I could ever fix this?"

My body shook with silent sobs. Everything I wanted. He was everything I wanted. He'd said everything I'd wanted to hear. My heart didn't feel like it had been broken, it felt as if it had been shredded. Horrible, deep, jagged tears that were causing me physical pain.

I felt his hand on my shoulder, I felt him slowly turn me, and pull me into a hug. I couldn't help myself, I leaned into him, breathing in the familiar scent that I missed so much. I gave myself a few seconds, before gently pushing myself away.

"You hurt me. You did worse than just breaking my heart. You broke me. I thought I wasn't worth it. I thought I was unlovable. I thought I wanted an armful of cats, because I was terminally single. I went to a very dark place. It took a long time before I saw light, but even with the light there were shadows of dark. Shadows that were made up of me missing you so freaking much. Shadows that just had to stay on the edges of my life. Shadows of pain, constantly there, constantly telling me that I wasn't enough. You didn't even text. Not even a 'hi'. You were able to walk away from me. So you read my blog? Well, congrats. You know that I was able to move on from you."

I stepped backwards, turned, and once again, walked away from the man I had thought would be my forever.

Chapter 16

I spent the weekend in bed. I got up to feed the cats, go to the bathroom, and eat. That was it. Otherwise I spent the weekend curled up in a ball crying. My eyes felt gritty and swollen from the tears. My heart and my head both ached.

By Sunday night, the tears and wine had left me feeling numb. It was if my head had been filled with a fog that removed all feelings, all emotion.

When I went to work on Monday, I felt I'd pulled it together. I did my best to walk through the day with my head held high. Around 1:00pm, I heard a knock on the door. I looked up and saw our administrative assistant, Cassie, at my door with a small vase holding one single, light pink rose. She also brought a small card.

I opened it up and saw Craig's familiar handwriting. I threw away the card right away, and then continued my work. However in the back of my mind, all I could think about was the card in the trash bin under my desk. I growled and retrieved it after a long fifteen minutes.

"Different colored roses have different meanings. I couldn't find one that could accurately portray how devastated and sorry I am. But this one, light pink, it means sympathy. I am hoping you will have sympathy and maybe let me see you. I love you."

Oh, Craig. Where were you? Where were these beautiful things even five weeks ago? I started to throw the letter away again, but stopped myself, instead deciding to slip it in my left hand drawer. I leaned forward to sniff the pretty flower. I caught myself smiling. He knew me too well. I would have been really angry if he'd gotten me a huge bouquet. That just meant guilt. Or cheating.

I shook my head and got back to work.

The next day, around the same time, another knock on the door and another single rose in a vase. This time a really pretty yellow flower. I set it on my desk next to the pink one. I set the card on my desk, trying to tell myself that I didn't need to read it right away. I went back to work, but had to stop to move the card a little closer to my computer monitor. You know, in case it decided to run away.

I managed to hold off for an hour this time. I mentally gave myself a high five before opening the card.

"A yellow rose signifies friendship. You have been my very best friend for over three years. Before we dated, you were already

someone incredibly special to me. I have missed my best friend. I love you."

I missed you too, Craig. A deep, soulful sigh, and I found myself raising the card to my nose to see if I could smell even the slightest hint of his cologne. I realized what I was doing, and mentally gave myself a shake. I opened the drawer and tossed the card in with its friend. I swear, I didn't check the drawer about five times to look at his handwriting. I also didn't run my fingers over the familiar chicken scratch, to feel closer to him. I really didn't.

Yeah. I really did.

Sniffle.

Wednesday at 1:00pm I was waiting for Cassie. 1:15pm came around, and I was getting antsy. 1:30pm and I was feeling depressed as all hell. I guess no more roses.

At 1:45pm there was a knock on my door. Cassie stood there looking frazzled. She held in her hand a single dark pink rose in its vase.

"Ash, really sorry. I got so backed up, and that asshole in marketing was chewing me out for about thirty minutes over an ad proof he says I didn't submit in time; when he never gave it to me. Anyway, here you go."

She plunked my vase down hard enough that the water sloshed on to my desk. I quickly moved my papers and that day's card out of the way. I raised an eyebrow at her in question.

"Oh, man. I'm sorry. It's just…it's just that man makes me want to see if the building is high enough to be worth jumping off of, sometimes. I'll get something to clean up the mess." Her shoulders were hunched forward in defeat. I made a mental note to talk to the marketing VP that had been giving her a hard time.

"No worries, Cass, I've got this."

She gave me a small smile of gratitude as she turned to return to her cubical.

I smiled at my new rose, and lined it up next to the other two.

"A dark pink rose means appreciation. Ash, I have always appreciated you and all you have always done for me. Maybe I wasn't always great at letting you know that, but given the chance, I will never let you forget it. I love you."

Damn, he was playing hard ball. I could lie and say that tears didn't come to my eyes a little, but what would be the point? I wiped at my eyes, kissed the card and put it away with the others.

"I love you, too." I thought to myself, not ready to say it out loud. Not ready to admit that the feelings I've always had for him were still there. I really needed to hold on to my angry, if only for a little bit longer.

Thursday came and around 12:56pm I walked up to the front, just to see if I could catch a glimpse of Craig. As I turned the corner, I saw him walking back out the front door and turning down the side walk. I heard Cassie getting up from her chair, and not wanting to get caught stalking my (ex)boyfriend, I turn to rush back to my office.

At least that was the plan.

I turned and started to run, but in turning my heel got caught up in the cheap carpeting and I pitched forward. I put my hands out in front of me and was able to keep from face planting on the ground. I stayed down for a second or two assessing whether I'd managed to hurt myself. Other than what felt like a skinned knee and a definite bruise to my ego, I pushed myself up. When I was standing, I saw Cassie standing there smirking at me, holding out my flower.

I snatched it from her, and pivoted to walk away.

"Black lace, huh? Hot date tonight?"

It was at that moment I realized that when I fell, my skirt landed in a manner that showed off my super sassy black lace undies. I normally would NOT wear these to work, but I hadn't exactly been feeling the best this week, so laundry and housework was not exactly my priority. As a result, my 'hot date' undies were being worn to the office.

"I could forget to pay you this week..." I did my best threatening voice, as my face turned bright red.

"Ooooh, I'm shaking." She laughed as she walked away.

I tried to be annoyed, but as the scent of the beautiful lavender rose filled my senses, I could do nothing but grin like an idiot.

Sitting down at my desk, I opened the card.

"Lavender roses apparently mean enchantment, or love at first sight. Both of these make me think of you. I have been enchanted with you since the day we met. Whether that qualifies as 'love at first

sight' or not, I don't know. But I know I haven't stopped being enchanted. I love you."

Wow. Enchanted. That's as awesome as someone telling me that they found me intriguing. Not being sarcastic, I had a guy once tell me that he found me intriguing and I was a goner. One more sniff of the rose, and it joined its friends. I was surprised that the Monday rose was still holding up pretty well.

The roses were starting to attract attention from the other women in the office, who were suspiciously walking by my office every day around 2:00pm. I had a feeling that Cassie may have been talking about the daily flowers I was receiving. I have to admit, the looks of jealousy made me very, very happy. Hey, don't judge! I figured I had earned that after what had been going on. Although, I wasn't feeling as betrayed as I had been. I was still hurt, but not as betrayed. Baby steps.

My phone chirped. I figured it was probably Craig, and I was excited, but not sure I was ready. I mean, I loved that he was trying to win me back, but wasn't one hundred percent sure I was ready to go back.

"I'm sorry." Huh, it was from Alex. With the fun I'd been having getting the flowers, I hadn't thought about her. How did I feel about her?

I was mad. I was still really mad. I don't know why she thought she had the right to dictate the path of my life. What made her think she could decide when I was ready to have my boyfriend back?

I was rational enough to know she hadn't set out to hurt me. Her intentions were fine, but she really went about it all in the worst possible way.

I thought about my response to her for a while.

"I know. But not ready yet."

I hoped that let her know to give me time, but that I understood nothing she did was out of any level of malice.

I missed my friends. With Alex and I not exactly communicating, none of us had spent any time together. Probably a good thing for my liver, as I had not consumed nearly the amount of red wine as I normally do.

Sigh. Seriously. A big, heavy, heartfelt sigh.

'chirp'

"'Kay, love you."

I had to smile. That was so Alex of her. Oh well, not ready yet. I shook the cobwebs out of my mind, and went back to work.

***

It was finally Friday. The week seemed to drag on and on, brightened only by the rainbow of roses I had on my desk. The day seemed to be running in slow motion, waiting for one o'clock to come around and find out what color of rose I would get.

Finally, I heard the tap on my door, but was surprised that instead of one rose, Cassie poked her head around and walked in with two roses in one little vase. Red and White.

Well, that was a change.

"Have you forgiven him yet?"

"Huh?"

I wanted to tear the card open and find out what he had written this time. I wanted to hold the flowers close and inhale their beautiful scent. I couldn't do this with Cassie standing there staring at me.

"Have. You. Forgiven. Him. Yet?" She annunciated each word as if I was hard of hearing, or a little slow, or both. "He comes by every day at 12:55pm, he has the same sad, lonely, haunted look on his face as he drops the flower of the day off. 'For Ashley', he says every time, before turning and leaving. That's all. So something happened, he's trying to get you back. Have you forgiven him?"

"Almost. I'm almost there."

"You may want to hurry up, because a guy like that won't stay single for long."

A sharp pang hit my heart. I hadn't even thought about what it would mean if I let him go. Someone else would get him. Someone else would hold his hand. Someone else would be showing him how to use Instagram. Someone else would have him making a fire in the fireplace for her, so that they could indulge in a romantic cuddle. Someone else. Not me.

I suddenly had a hard time breathing. Tears were filling my eyes. Tears that I couldn't allow to spill over. I was at work and needed to pull it together.

I pulled out the card, and when I opened it up, I saw that it was much longer than the rest.

"Deep red means willingness for commitment, deep passion. White alone means purity and everlasting love. When you bring a

*red and a white rose together, it means unity. Two completely
separate things can be something incredible when brought together.
That's us. We are something incredible when we are together. We
are something completely different when we are apart.*

*I miss you, Ashley. I miss how you hide behind your fingers
when there's a gory scene in a TV show that I'm watching. I miss
how you clean up after me, even when I'm not done making the
mess. I miss watching you dancing and singing around the living
room when cleaning, when you don't think anyone is there. I miss
cuddling with you on the couch, feeling you breathe. I even miss
when you wake up and try to hide the drool that you left on my shirt.*

*I will wait for you. Because we are worth waiting for. I'm
beyond sorry that I walked away like I did. I'm sorry I hurt you with
my words. I'm sorry I went along with Alex's crazy idea. Now,
looking back, I can see it was a pretty dumb thing to do. But at the
time, I would have done anything for you, even following your
friend's dumb plan and staying away.*

*You are the most incredible part of my life. You are the reason I
smile during the day.*

*I want back in. I'm not done. We are nowhere near done.
Please, let me know you still love me.*

I'd like to see you go from singleish to foreverish. I love you."
Forever.

That was the thing I wanted. I wanted forever. I wanted the
freaking fairytale.

I set the new roses in line with the others and snapped a picture.
The one from Monday was starting to wilt a bit, so I figured it was
time to start drying out some of the roses.

When I went home I sat on the couch, surrounded as always
with my furry family.

I leaned my head back on the couch, just so confused as to what
I wanted. I tried to imagine my life without Craig in it permanently. I
mean, I knew what it was like to live without him. I obviously had
done so for the past seven weeks. But, I'd spent those past seven
weeks not willing to think of a life without him. I closed my eyes
and tried to imagine moving on, finding someone else. I pictured
going on a real first date with someone other than Craig. When it
came time in my mind for the good night kiss, I started crying again.

I couldn't do it. I couldn't walk away from us. Yeah, I was still hurting, but I couldn't say goodbye.

A crash had me nearly jumping out of my skin. I looked towards where the noise was and saw Penny, standing over a photo frame she'd knocked over. I picked it up and found myself looking at a picture of Craig and me. We were side by side, at a friend's party. I was looking at the camera and trying to smile all seriously, while he was busy nuzzling my neck. I remembered that day, he'd been attempting to grow out a goatee or something so his scruffiness was tickling my neck. We got about two decent 'couple' shots from that day, but this one had always been my favorite. Craig and I being a normal couple. I knew what I had to do. I just hoped he'd get the message.

I pulled out the laptop and logged into the blog. Alex and Craig said that he'd been following it during the experiment. Well, now was the time to find out if he really had. I chose the option to write a new blog, and started typing.

"This has been a crazy journey. It started with careless words. 'I'm done'. Words that mean one thing to him, and another to me. And after the words – silence. Silence for six weeks while I worked through the pain and the feelings of being abandoned. Six weeks where I had some strange adventures that would have been even more strange – and wonderful – with him by my side.

Life was not meant to be lived alone. I would complete a fun 'assignment' from my friends and the first thing I'd do was pick up my phone to tell him about it. But he was gone. The last I'd heard from him, he was on a 'work trip' and wouldn't be back for two weeks.

Blog class ended last week and yet I received an assignment to go sing Karaoke. I don't do public speaking. I certainly don't do public singing. Unless there's alcohol. Lots of alcohol…and a group of equally inebriated women around me. I said no way. She said 'I dare you'. So I went. I belted that bitch out and gave it all the sass. I was singing my song to him. I was picturing myself singing it to him in the car, and it was so real, I could feel his hand on mine. But it wasn't real.

As I went to leave, he was there. He knew I'd be there. I had been set up. It turned out, he had been kept from me. My friend Alex thought I needed to go through this experience alone. I needed to have some adventures alone to be able to appreciate the adventures together. To better appreciate him. To appreciate us.

I won't lie. I lost it. I yelled, I cried, I ran. I was done. Again, those words. Those careless, painful words. 'I'm done.'

But then the rainbow happened. At one o'clock every afternoon, the rainbow started appearing. Different color roses, just one per day. Each color a different meaning. Each color a request for forgiveness. Each color chipping away at my pain, laying me raw and exposed. Each color breaking down my resolve to stay angry just a little bit longer.

I was told today, that I should make up my mind about forgiving him, because someone else would be more than willing to snap him up and keep him as their own. I was not thinking about someone else. I did not like this someone else. As a matter of fact, whoever she is out there, waiting to jump in and take my place, she can suck it.

I'm not ready to be a half of anything other than us. So, I choose 'us'.

Are you reading this? Are you catching on? I'm ready to not be angry. I'm ready to be us.

Come home."

With that, I uploaded a picture of the six roses, and clicked 'post'.

And waited.

And waited.

Waited.

I looked at the clock and realized it was already ten o'clock at night. Disappointed, I realized that he probably wouldn't be reading the post tonight. I started turning off the lights and made my way up the stairs to the bedroom. When I heard it. A light knock on the door. Had I imagined it? A second, much louder knock rang through the silent house.

I ran down the stairs and unlocked the door. Pulling the door open I saw a very disheveled Craig standing at the door. He looked as if he'd lost weight since last Friday. There were dark circles under his eyes, and his cheeks looked a little sunken in. I looked into those beautiful brown eyes I'd dreamt of, I saw unshed tears. I saw hope. I saw love.

I launched myself at him, and he held me close as we both started sobbing. I heard his deep, rumbling voice whisper in my ear: "Ash, I'm home."

Epilogue – Three months later

I wrapped my arms around myself as I watched the moving van pull away from the house. I tried not to cry. I tried not to feel anything. No emotions, emotions were silly right now. But I sniffed, and wiped at a tear impatiently. The van turned the corner and pulled out of view.

I turned to walk back into my house, and was met at the door by the love of my life. He wrapped his arms around me and kissed the top of my head.

"Why the tears, Ash?"

I looked at him and just smiled.

"I can't believe you have finally moved in."

"Didn't I promise forever?"

"Uh, no…you promised foreverish! Big difference, buddy. Big freaking difference."

"Whatever."

He knew I hated whatever, so I poked him in the ribs, hitting him in a very ticklish spot. He swatted at me, so I did it again, and again. Suddenly, I was airborne. Oops! I found myself slung over his shoulder with a lovely view of his butt. A lovely upside-down view. Who cared, yummy.

He started running up the stairs with me and tossed me onto the bed that had just been added to my guest room. I mean, our guest room. Next thing I knew, my pants were being shimmied down my hips, and tossed into a corner. I sat up and pushed away a little.

"What on earth are you doing?"

"You need to ask? I must not be doing it right if you need to ask."

"Okay, I totally know what you are doing, but why?"

"We need to christen this bed. We've christened the couch, your bed, the counter, the kitchen table, the bathroom sink."

"Yeah, don't remind me. I'll probably have a bruise on my back from the faucet for more than a week."

"So, now it's time to christen my old bed. Well, time to christen it in this house, anyway."

With that, he crawled up and straddled my hips, pinning me to the bed. He leaned forward and cupped my cheek gently with his hand.

He leaned forward and gave me a toe-curling, mind numbing kiss.

"I love you, Ashley. I appreciate you. You are my best friend. I am enchanted by you." He was repeating the roses to me. Okay, no more resistance. I flipped him over and straddled him, kissing him thoroughly while starting to remove his clothes. Good thing I didn't have anything planned for a while, this was not going to be a quickie.

***

We flopped back on the bed, completely exhausted from crazy, monkey marathon sex.

He reached over to put his arm around me and I slapped him away.

"No! Tired. Bed."

He laughed at me, pulled me close and started snoring before I even closed my eyes.

What seemed like minutes later, I heard him moaning. I opened my eyes and watched him as he was wriggling around and looked like he was in ecstasy.

"Oh yeah, oh God, yesssss. Oh baby, that is amazing. Mmmmmm. I guess you weren't that tired, were you?"

I was really confused, this was one hell of a dream he was having.

I looked down his body, past his waist and yelped when I saw what was going on.

Midnight, the black kitten who was no longer a kitten, was…um..giving his daddy a bath.

"Midnight, noooo!" I tried to whisper as I swiped my hand at him.

Craig chose that moment to fully wake up and open his eyes.

"Honey, why did you stop?" He looked down and into the golden eyes of a kitty that was about to take another lick.

"WHAT THE HELL!" Midnight jumped up in the air about three feet, turned and hauled ass out of the room.

I was dying. Absolutely dying. Bent over in half on the bed, tears rolling down my face, dying.

The look of shock and horror on Craig's face was priceless. Oh my God, I wish I'd had a camera. Or video. Or both.

I bit my lip. I seriously was going to have to write this one up.

"Don't you even think about it!"

"About what?" I batted my eyes, attempting my best innocent look.

"I know you. You wanted to blog it. Well, first, you wanted to video tape it. But then you were totally thinking about writing about it and sharing with the world that I just got serviced by a cat. A male cat. The answer is not just no, but HELL no."

Crap. He is good.

He gave me the most solemn look.

"We shall never speak of this again."

"Uh-huh, okay." Yeah, we were totally going to speak of this again. "Well, I guess life isn't too boring around here anymore."

"Honey, with you, nothing is, or ever has been boring.

I smiled, leaning back into his arms, sighing contentedly.

"So, who's better?"

"Huh?"

"Me or Midnight. Who is better?"

I waited for his response.

I leaned up on an elbow and looked at him. Nothing.

I poked him in the ribs.

"What? I'm thinking?"

Like hell he was getting time to think about that.

With that I pounce on him like a cat and start tickling him until he begged for mercy. And some other stuff. He begged for a bunch of other stuff, too. Yummy!

The End. Or maybe…The Beginning.

###

Acknowledgements

A special thanks to A. E. Murphy. I started out reading her book, "Broken", and was hooked. It was the first time I'd emailed an author after reading one of her books. That single email a little over a year ago turned into a friendship I truly treasure. She asked me to be a beta reader, then she asked my opinions when mulling over some content decisions. She kept pushing me and pushing me to write. She kept telling me that I had what it takes to write a book. I will forever be grateful that I tried to prove her wrong.

To my awesome beta ladies: Mom, Nikki, Amy, Rachel and Andrea. I really appreciate you guys reading this little book and giving your honest feedback. I could have re-read Singleish fifty times and not found every little problem. Thank you so much, guys, for helping me with my baby!

About the Author

I'm thirty seven years old, and this is my first book, ever. I've tried to write before. I would sit down, all serious, fingers to the keyboard and would pound out the next great American novel. And I would fill exactly one page. Yup. Just one.

I've been reading for as long as I can remember. Before I can remember, actually. Mom tells me that I was reading the newspaper to them when I was only three years old.

I've been blessed to marry an incredible man who was kind enough to put up with me ignoring him while I wrote this book, and was even kinder to read it and give feedback. Together we have twelve rescued pets. I had the opportunity to work at an animal shelter in a past life, and one of the occupational hazards of working at an animal shelter is you end up with a LOT of animals.

My mom and dad never doubted that I had this book in me. Mom always wanted me to be a published author. Well, Mom, it looks like I did it!

I really don't know what else to write…so I'll just say thank you, again.

Adopt, don't shop.

Want to know more about me? Check out my Smashwords interview:

https://www.smashwords.com/interview/ebutts422

Connect with Elizabeth Butts

Thank you so much for taking the time out of your day/week/life to read Singleish. It means so much to me that you trusted your free time to my ramblings. I would love to hear from you! Here's how to connect with me online:

Follow me on Facebook:
https://www.facebook.com/ElizabethButtsAuthor

Check out my blog:
https://elizabethbuttsauthor.wordpress.com/

Email me: ebutts422@gmail.com

Favorite me at Smashwords:
https://www.smashwords.com/profile/view/ebutts422

Made in the USA
Middletown, DE
07 September 2015